This is a work of fiction. Names, characters, businesses, places, events and incidents are either the products of the author's imagination or used in a fictitious manner. Any resemblance to actual persons, living or dead, or actual events is purely coincidental.

ISBN **978-1-943159-19-2**

LCCN 2019907534

The publisher would appreciate notification where errors occur so that they may be corrected in subsequent printing and/or editions. Please send comments to the publisher by emailing to deeprivers67@yahoo.com

Printed in the United States of America

Dedication Page:

 I want to dedicate this book to all the strong women in my life. Without you, I wouldn't be the man I am today. Your strength, power, love, compassion, encouragement, praise, spirituality and womanly obedience has been a blessing to encounter.

Decisions 2 True Adjustments

By: Ralph M Edgerson Jr

INTRO

After three years the Daniels family gets to celebrate a few accomplishments as Alonna puts the finishing touches on her upcoming wedding to her fiancé Steven, Kareem starts up a new adventure with a new clippers and hair product line called "Hard Head", Shalay and Kevin became business partners of a new hotel maid service "NOLA Maids" and Sherell gets ready with Cedric to send out the birthday cards for their son Tre's "Terrible Two" birthday party. It all was picture perfect, a true TV family moment as everything was coming together so well but tragedy will hit this family so hard that it will rock them to the core, where morals and values will be questioned.

CHAPTER 1

Cedric, Tre and Lamaj were heading home from Lamaj's football

practice when his mom Delores called.

"Hey old lady", answered Cedric as he turned into the driveway.

"I don't wanna talk to you. Where my babies at, Sherell said they were

with you", replied Delores.

Cedric listened to his mother as she went on about how she wants all of

her grandkids at church Sunday because the church is holding its 27th

annual fair after service. Cedric agreed to bring the boys to church this

Sunday to enjoy the festivities with the rest of the family. Delores told

Cedric that her oldest grandsons, Devin and Khori, are coming in town

from college for that same weekend to be with the family.

Cedric was excited to see his nephews because he hadn't seen them since they both went off to college except for seeing Devin at his college football games in Texas. Devin was a top prospect at the defensive end position when he was a junior in college but he wanted to finish and graduate with a degree in business management before he pursued a football career. He was so proud of his nephew for making that choice. Khori on the other hand became fascinated with growing plants that he studied to become a botanist and has less than a year to finish with a degree in Botany. Lamaj was Devin's biggest fan when it came to football that he even played the same position at his school. He was even more excited to see his adopted cousins come back in town when Cedric told him about their upcoming visit. Sherell heard her three men walk in the house and Tre went straight to his favorite toys on the floor as Lamaj made his way to the refrigerator like any other teen would when they first come inside. Sherell looked at her son,

"Boy if you don't get upstairs and get in the shower. Funkin' up my kitchen."

Cedric laughed, "I didn't wanna say anything dude but you are ripe."

Lamaj closed the refrigerator door, "Dang, ok I'm going. I'm going."

He headed upstairs while Cedric began to tell Sherell about the request Delores put in for the boys to be with her at church Sunday.

"Yeah, I talked to Alonna earlier today. We all going, you included sir", replied Sherell. Cedric tried to talk himself out of the event,

"Baby, the game coming on. My mama church be hot."

"The devil always hot when he in church", giggled Sherell.

"Oh you got jokes", responded Cedric as he walked up to Sherell.

"But I love my little devil", replied Sherell while giving her man a kiss.

As the two engaged into a passionate kiss, Cedric's cell started ringing,

"Dammit I can't even get a quickie in."

Cedric's attorney was calling and Sherell headed upstairs as she gave him his phone. Cedric's attorney called to let him know that Denise has yet to sign their divorce papers. The situation has been frustrating Cedric for the past two months now since he officially went through every tedious request Denise's attorney has brought to the table. Cedric's vexation spilled through the phone,

"I've done everything they have asked! She said we got the house together, so I sold it and we split the money 50/50. I gave her the damn car

I bought for her. The kid is not mine, so I know damn well she ain't asking for child support. What else does she want? Why the fuck she ain't sign it yet?"

Cedric's attorney completely understood his clients gripe but had no answers for him,

"Maybe you could bring the papers to her personally and get her to sign them. But Ced, I need you to be calm, cool and collective when talking to her. We don't need this stretched out any longer than it has to be, ok. Now I can send a courier over tomorrow or you can come pick up the paperwork Monday morning."

Cedric agreed to picking the papers up Monday morning because Lamaj has a game Saturday afternoon and he doesn't want to miss it. The two gentlemen concluded their call and Cedric turned around to a concern faced Lamaj,

"You ok? I heard you all the way upstairs."

"I'm good Manny, nothing I can't handle", replied Cedric.

Yolanda was in her office finishing her daily attendance when the school secretary called over the speakerphone,

"Ms. Patton, a Mr. Daniels is here for you."

Yolanda told her to send him to her office as she filed away her paperwork. Kareem walked in,

"Ms. Patton, I'm here for my detention. I've been very bad."

Yolanda smiled as she seen her handsome lover stand in the doorway waiting for her response. She got up from her desk, walked over to him and they kissed as if they haven't seen each other in days.

"I need to call you Ms. Patton more often if I can get this kind of treatment all the time", stated Kareem as he glanced over his sexy queen.

Yolanda grabbed her jacket as Kareem picked up her briefcase and they headed to the front door,

"Mama Dee called me today and told me she wants to see the both of us at church Sunday and not just for the fair afterwards. All I could say was 'Yes ma'am' cause she was serious. You know yo mama don't play."

Kareem started laughing cause he knew it was true,

"When that lady mind is set on something she will not let up. Now she told me this morning about Sunday. I guess she was making sure I show up."

The couple was driving home after a long day but Yolanda wanted to stop by her sister to check on her because she hadn't heard from Denise all week,

"Baby, you can go home and I'll go over there by myself. You don't have to come."

"It's no biggie, I'll go baby. Unless yo secret boyfriend over there and you don't want me to see him", joked Kareem as Yolanda gave him an evil look and sarcastically responded,

"He won't be there. He's with one of your THOTS."

They both clowned around as Kareem parked in front of Denise's apartment. Kareem waited outside and made a few calls to his shops while Yolanda went to go see her little sister.

Yolanda and Kareem seemed to have an understanding when it comes to Denise. He doesn't care much about Denise after what all has happened between her and his brother but he also knows the strength of a sibling bond and he respects that. Kareem sat in the car with the radio playing while he watched rambunctious pre-teens laugh as they run zig zags across the busy street of Tchoupitoulas causing drivers to brake and blow their horns at them.

"These lil fools gone get they self hit", laughed Kareem as he remembered he use to like being that silly when he was little.

He sat there reminiscing over old days of him and Cedric running through New Orleans East playing ball at Joe Brown Park and chasing little girls around. While Kareem was going down memory lane, an upset Yolanda walked up, got in and immediately started venting about her visit with Denise. She started with how distant Denise was with her when she first walked in. Yolanda went on talking about how Denise began fussing about Cedric and the divorce paperwork,

"She said, Cedric needs to pay her some sort of alimony because they were together when he moved up in position and she has grown accustom to a certain lifestyle."

Kareem was confused on the matter,

"But she got pregnant for another dude. How she expects to get money from her ex to take care of another man's child?"

"Exactly, that's what I mentioned and that's when the argument started. I tried to tell her she was wrong but of course she brought up our relationship and I was done after that. All I wanted to do then was see my niece and go home", replied Yolanda.

Kareem drove a bit longer, as Yolanda was till angered over the situation

with her sister, he pulled up to their house and the two went in for the

night.

CHAPTER 2

It was early Saturday morning and Lamaj was doing his normal routine he always does the morning of a game. He made himself a big breakfast; eggs, sausage, grits, bacon, toast and a large cup of his orange juice and cranberry juice mix. After breakfast he went out to the backyard and went through a rigorous routine of defensive schemes, moves, run sprints and magnificent vertical leaps. Lamaj was sitting down catching his second wind when he heard a voice behind him,

"You tired already youngin'? We didn't go head to head yet."

When he turned around Devin was standing there in his college sweats ready to practice with his little cousin and show him some new tricks of the trade. The boys hugged each other and instantly engaged into a barrage of hand-to-hand football combat, moving sporadically around the yard like two elite martial artists with all intent to better the other with some kind of advance. Devin chuckled as he seen his little cousin's skills have gotten much better since their last encounter,

"Looka you bringing that work, you got some nice hand and foot skills cuz. I don't think they ready for you today, ya heard me."

"I thought you wasn't coming in town until late tonight", stated Lamaj.

Devin let him know he couldn't miss another game and that statement right there made Lamaj's day. Win, lose or draw he knew today he was going to play the hardest he's ever played and leave it all on the field. The two went inside so Lamaj could get ready and ran into Sherell in the kitchen,

"Hey Devin, you just get in? You want some breakfast? Cause yo buddy left everything out on the counter, like he has a maid."

Devin laughed but declined the offer as Lamaj darted upstairs to his room to avoid his mother's wrath. Cedric and Tre came downstairs,

"What's good Dev, you just get in?"

"Yeah, I had to see my cuz play today. That boy is getting big and he solid like a brick wall", responded Devin.

They all sat in the kitchen as Devin laughed at his youngest cousin Tre's antics as Sherell frantically tried to get her toddler to eat his pancakes. After Tre finally finished his food everybody started to get ready for the game in a few hours.

Shalay called her twin to see if her nephew Devin made it in town yet,

"Girl, Khori over here eating everything in sight like he don't eat at all."

"Don't do my baby like that, you know that cafeteria food is nasty", replied Alonna.

Khori confirmed his aunt's assumptions,

"That stuff in the cafeteria is so bland, I keep a bottle of hot sauce in my backpack. I haven't had a good hot meal in a minute."

Even though Shalay would never take offense to any of her kids raiding her fridge she had to mess with her first college kid. Shalay was so proud of her firstborn and all his siblings knew he was the standard they had to live up to. Shalay's second oldest Ronnisha didn't mind the challenge of being as good or better than her big brother. Ronnisha was already on her way as a junior in high school with honors classes and college credits already. She also goes to NOCCA, New Orleans Center of Creative Arts, where she is a talented painter with artwork in a several corporate offices. But she truly looks up to Khori because he encourages her every chance he gets to push harder with all she does. Ronnisha loves hanging with Khori and she meant he wasn't leaving her sight this weekend. As soon as he finished eating, Khori told his mom he was heading out for a drive and Ronnisha invited herself,

"Mama I'm going with Khori."

"Who said you was coming bighead?", asked Khori as he knew his little sister wasn't leaving his side.

Ronnisha gave Khori a "I ain't paying attention to nothing you saying" look, got in the car and put on her seat-belt,

"We going or what bruh?"

Khori got in, "Yo ass a mess for real" as he started the engine.

Alonna and Steven were going over their guest list for what Steven felt was the 100th time,

"Baby do we really have to go through this again? I mean as long as you tell me what time to be there and you standing at the alter is all that matters. Why do we have to go over this again?"

Alonna's response intimidated Steven into submission,

"Boy if you don't sit down and go over this list with me. You wanna pay for people who not coming? I'm trying to save you money, I'm trying to help you out."

As they went over the names Alonna seen she had Denise's name on the list,

"Nope that's not about to happen, delete."

Steven laughed aloud as he knew Denise is one person that would never be allowed at her wedding. Yolanda on other hand has made it to be her second Maid of Honor only second to Sherell. The three women never realized how much they had in common until Yolanda and Kareem became an item. Usually during the weekend Alonna, Sherell and Yolanda make it a point to hook up either in person to do some "retail therapy" or on the phone to chop it up. They all have a man in their lives that simply adore them and is not ashamed to show the world. Alonna jokes with her brothers that soon after her wedding that they would probably be next to get married. Kareem always claim Shalay needs to be the next up to the alter in that matter. Cedric really considered getting engaged to Sherell but he wanted to finalize his divorce first before he popped the question to her. As Alonna went thru the last few names of her list her baby girl Dashanae came running,

"Mama mama! Devin here! He just pulled up."

Dashanae loved her big brother especially cause she would see him on TV when the college football games came on.

"Hey mama, what's up Steven", stated Devin as he made his way in the room where Alonna and Steven was sitting with a bunch of papers in front of them,

"What is all this?"

"Ya mama mountain of 'Steven To Do List' or else", replied Steven as he got up to greet Devin, "How you been homie?"

Steven been in Devin's life 14 of the 21 years he's been on this earth and he's truly the only father he knows because his biological father died before Semaj was born. Steven never really wanted Devin or Semaj to call him dad because he always told them,

"I could never replace your dad and I would never try to. He was taken away from you and he wanted to be a part of your life but what I can do is stand in as a sub to honor his wishes as a father, cause that's what you deserve."

Devin and Steven have had their ups and downs but they have always come back together as a team. Alonna loved the fact that they had such a strong bond because she never wanted her boys to think she was replacing their father with someone else. Devin came over to get dressed for the high school football game and take Semaj and Dashanae with him to watch Lamaj play.

"Where they playing at today?", asked Alonna.

"Khori texted me that it's gonna be at Tad Gormley Stadium, he and Ronnisha gone meet us there", replied Devin.

Alonna's kids headed out the door as she was letting them know that dinner would be ready when they all get back,

"Y'all come back hungry cause Steven throwing some burgers on the grill."

As Dashanae was getting in the car she turned to her mom,

"Mama tell me you making the potato salad cause daddy puts too much mustard is his. Like every time."

Alonna burst out laughing,

"Girl don't let yo daddy hear you talk about his food. You know he think he's a gourmet chef in here."

Devin drove off and headed up the street to the stadium to meet up with Khori.

Yolanda was sitting in the living room reading one of her favorite erotic novels when Kareem came in from running errands earlier this morning,

"Hey you. What you doing sexy?"

"Waiting on you to do me like this man did this women in this book", replied Yolanda as she put the book down, kissed Kareem on the lips and grabbed a handful of semi-hard dick waiting for her in his sweat pants.

Kareem picked Yolanda up off her feet and she wrapped her legs around him as their tongues twist and twirl around one another. Yolanda's fingers just ran threw his dreads as Kareem walked to the bedroom. Kareem laid her on the bed, began sliding her leggings down as Yolanda snatched her top off and he just stopped for a minute to admire this thick caramel honey laying on the bed waiting for his pleasure. She noticed him just gazing at her and couldn't help but to ask,

"What are you looking at?"

"My lunch and dinner", replied Kareem as he went head first between her legs, onto her freshly waxed pussy and began licking her clit with the tip of his tongue.

Yolanda's legs set perfectly on top of his shoulders, positioning her saturated monkey completely in his mouth. But then Kareem pulled her closer to him and shoved his tongue deep inside her extracting a squirm and exhaling moan from Yolanda. Her juices started to flow out and Kareem's tongue attempted to catch every drip as his tongue twirled around her thumping clitoris. She could feel that first orgasm approach as chills began to electrify her body,

"No not yet."

She wanted to enjoy his oral pleasuring a little longer but Kareem knew his woman's body, his tongue sped up in motion as she couldn't hold on any longer and exploded in his mouth while holding tight on his head. Yolanda's shivers was almost calming down when she could feel his dick head part her lips and slide deep inside her,

"Oh my goodness! You Muthafucka!" was the only logical thing to say when she felt him begin to stroke. It felt like Kareem was deep in her stomach every time he pushed in but she absorbed every thrust and welcomed another with every moan she let out. Yolanda's big full breast bounced and jiggled with every impact as the sounds of an unceasing flow of juices filled the room while Kareem forcibly pound away to Yolanda's second orgasm. Kareem knew he couldn't last much longer with how good Yolanda's soft wet pussy felt on his dick, so he did the one thing that he knew would give him a little more time with this delicious juice box. He pulled out and began eating her pussy all over again but this time he opened her lips, pushed back her clitoral hood and sucked on her exposed clit sending her into ecstasy. Right when Yolanda was about to cum for the third time he knew it was his chance to finish the job. He turned Yolanda on her side, opened her legs and they got in "The Pretzel" position. The couple simultaneously peaked as the intense performance went from rapid fire jabs to a slow stroke motion. They simply collapsed into each other breathing heavily as they embraced the euphoria surrounding their bodies.

"I came in here to tell you something but I forgot", smiled Kareem as he just rubbed on Yolanda's soft thighs.

She loved feeling his warm hands caress her body,

"You keep rubbing on me and we gone start round two."

Kareem's hands reached down between her legs and his fingers began to massage her still throbbing moist clit,

"Nuff said, let's go."

And the second round began.

Cedric, Sherell and Tre were getting their seats behind the team's bench as the crowd cheered when the players entered the field. Lamaj and his teammates made it to the bench and Tre stood up screaming his big brother's name so everyone could hear who number 57 was. Lamaj smiled at his little brother and made their signature Hulk move they have always done at every game which sent Tre into a frenzy of excitement. The ref blew the whistle and the kickoff started the game with a horde of teens charging toward one another. Devin and the crew all met up out front of the stadium, they could hear the game starting as the crowd roared,

"Man let's go we missing the game."

Khori was rushing through the front gate when he ran across a guy he recognized from school,

"What's good dude, you out here for the game?"

The pungent aroma of marijuana oozed from the guy's body and clothing,

"Something like that, what the hell you doing out here Kush? You do know Garu and his crew outchere right?"

"Don't call me Kush in front my peeps. I ain't frettin' Garu and none of his clowns, they know what it is", whispered Khori as he let his family walk ahead of him.

Ronnisha waited for her brother to catch up as she stood by gate C entrance,

"Why he call you Kush? Dude smelled like a pound of weed and who the hell is Garu?"

Khori brushed all his sister's questions off,

"Damn you be ear hustling. Can you stop asking me shit and let's go look at the game."

The group of cousins got right by the band as they enjoyed the game but Khori's head was on a swivel as his associate's comments echoed his memories. The band started their way to the field for the halftime show and Khori offered to get everyone some refreshments from the concession stand. As he walked through the crowd he seen an unwanted sight, Garu and three of his followers. Garu was a well known street dealer in New Orleans who went to college with Khori, he never really liked Khori because he felt Khori was disrupting his business and causing him to lose money. They've had a few physical encounters at school, nothing major that warrant instant aggression but Khori wasn't taking any chances. Khori stood in the crowd with his hands in his pockets, one hand clenching 100 dollars while the other one was wrapped around a fully loaded 9mm. He inched up as the crowd moved but trying not to make eye contact with Garu or any of his cronies. Khori made it to the stand, began making his order and that's when he noticed Garu had recognized him at the counter.

He prepared himself for the worst as he had a firm grip on his firearm, Garu was making his way straight toward him but then his eyes got wide as silver dollars and Garu turned around to walk away. Faith stepped in as three NOPD officers were escorting Khori's weed smelling associate through the crowd out of the stadium in handcuffs and caused Garu's instant retreat. Khori's grip loosened from his weapon as he grasped hold of the cart that held all the refreshments for his sister and cousins waiting on him in their seats. Khori started walking up the steps when he seen his uncle Cedric wave him over to him,

"Boy get over here!"

He seen his group had made their way down to Cedric and he made his way to them.

"What's going on Uncle Ced? I know that's not Lil Tre over there" stated Khori as he kissed Sherell on the cheek.

They all sat down to get ready for the second half of the game but Khori's eyes kept glancing over the crowd of football patrons looking for any sort of problems and no one had a clue of the anxiety he was going thru at the time.

Devin stood like a proud father as he watched his cousin Lamaj wreck havoc on the opposing team's offensive line. Double teams or switching players couldn't keep Lamaj away from making some kind of play on the ball. With four sacks, two tackles for a lost, two blocked passes and a fumble recovery for a touchdown everybody in the stadium knew who number 57 was and Devin roared as his cousin amazed the crowd with his athletic feats. Sherell was almost hoarse screaming her son's name every time he hit the field. The whole group was so excited to see how good Lamaj really was that they stood the whole second half. Lamaj's performance pushed his teammates to perform at the same level with Cornerbacks intercepting ill thrown passes, Running backs grinding out 45 yard touchdown runs and even a 95 yard kick return for a touchdown. All of their actions drove the team to a 42 to 17 victory over their opponent. Devin was in utter awe watching how well Lamaj performed on the field that he had to get down by the team to celebrate with them. Lamaj asked his coach could his cousin join them on the bench as the last few seconds clicked on the clock and after the coach noticed who Lamaj was referring to he welcomed the star athlete. As the clock struck zero the teams exited the field and all huddled around Devin as he went into "coach mode" letting the teens know how well they all did,

"I want you to remember this feeling. Remember your performance. That was not a weak team you just beat but you beat them all the same. Know that some days you're going to be outmatched and other days it's going to feel so easy. Soak in every detail coach teaches you, perfect it, perform it and even tweak it to adjust to your skill level but by all means listen to everything he has for you. Last but not least eat young bucks! Eat! Y'all did good today."

The team started chanting, "Eat! Eat! Eat!" as they jumped up and down on the field. The coach looked and realized he couldn't have given a better endgame speech for his team.

CHAPTER 3

Delores had on her Sunday's best accompanied with the matching wide floral hat and large floral purse as she walked into church greeting her Pastor at the door,

"Morning Pastor Jenkins."

"Morning Sister Daniels, how are we doing this beautiful morning?", replied Pastor Jenkins.

Delores let the Pastor know she's "blessed and highly favored" as she walked in to claim her seats for her soon arriving family members. As Delores made her way into the church she seen a sight that warmed her heart, all her children and grandkids were already seated waiting on her to sit with them. Tre ran up the aisle to his grandmother as fast as his chubby legs could take him,

"Maw Maw!", and hugged her so tight.

Kareem walked up to chaperon his mother to the pew where they all were sitting,

"Young lady you late. You gone have to explain where you been after service over with."

Delores smiled and took her seat as the matriarch glanced over her happy family, her day has been made wonderful. The congregation all gathered in and sat down as the Pastor confidently walked up to the podium,

"God is good."

The audience replied,

"All the time." The Pastor repeated,

"God is good!" The audience acknowledged again,

"All the time!"

As the Pastor went into his sermon it was as he was speaking to the Daniels family personally talking about family, love, betrayal, devotion, determination and sacrifice. They all felt and got something from today's speech as they welcomed Pastor's sermon.

Denise was sitting on the sofa with her active three year old daughter Ashley as Jamal walked in,

"Hey, what my pretty girls doing?" stated Jamal as he picked Ashley up to kiss her.

"It's pretty outside, you wanna go to the lake or something? Get out the house for awhile?", asked Jamal.

Denise really didn't want to go but she felt the outside adventure would be good for Ashley as she was running out of things to do inside. Jamal mentioned there was a big fair at a church that his nephew told him about,

"Maybe we could bring Ashley over there to have some fun, what you think?"

"If it's that church in the Lower 9th ward, no", replied Denise.

Jamal looked confused as he wondered why she wouldn't want to go to a church function,

"Why not, what's wrong with that church?"

Denise then let him know that that's the Daniels' family church and she knows they all would be there for the annual fair the church has every year. Jamal agreed they wouldn't have to go there and the two chose to go to the lake and relax with Ashley. He started getting his daughter's toys while Denise grabbed two large throw blankets to put in the car,

"You want me to make a few sandwiches for us", asked Denise.

Jamal suggested they stop by the po-boy shop on their way out,

"I could grab us some daiquiris too. You know you want one."

Denise laughed as she strapped Ashley in the car seat,

"You know I ain't saying no."

They headed out for a little family fun when Jamal's cell started ringing, it was his nephew on the other end asking if he was going to meet him at the fair . Jamal let his nephew know he's going to Lake Pontchartrain instead,

"You more than welcome to meet us out there, you know I'm a be in my usual spot."

Jamal looked after his nephew like he was his own son and they've made many trips to the lake so he knew exactly where the "usual spot" was but he told his uncle that he'll meet up with him after he and his friends stop by the church fair first.

Pastor Jenkins finished his sermon in a thankful prayer,

"Almighty Father we thank You for another day on this earth. We thank You for another chance to better ourselves as a people. We thank You for our family. We thank You for our children. We thank You for all Your blessings, all Your gifts and all Your help in all You do. We thank You for everything You have given us. In Jesus mighty name we pray. Amen."

The congregation all announced,

"Amen" and started to gather toward the aisles of the church as the ushers lead everyone to the exit doors.

Little Tre held his grandmother's hand as he walked with her to the large decorated open lot next to the church where he could see brightly colored banners stringed across the tall light poles and colorful balloons floating everywhere. His face lit up when he seen the clowns blowing balloons for the excited kids near by and the merry-go-round truly caught his attention with its shiny multi-colored horses. Delores just wanted to sit and relax but the look of pure joy on her youngest grandson's face was enough to push her to get on the merry-go-round with him. She was saved just in time by Dashanae,

"Grandma go chill with mama and auntie Shay, I'm a go with him. C'mon Tre let's go."

The little ones ran off to get in line as Delores made her way to the picnic table where her twin daughters were sitting waiting for her.

"Mama, you really was gonna get on that thing with him?", asked Shalay.

"I was gonna call one of y'all to come get him", giggled Delores.

The three relaxed at the table as they watched everyone enjoy the fair. People from all over the city came to enjoy the fair like they have for the past 27 years but they all stared in amazement when they seen brightly colored feathers in the distance make its way to the fair. Ronnisha went running to see the event because she knew exactly who it was, besides one thing she has to see every Mardi Gras or every Super Sunday is The Mardi Gras Indians, she truly loved seeing their colorful costumes and elaborate designs. The crowd gathered together when they heard a loud chant,

"The Chief is here! The Chief is here! Hey now Big Chief is here!"

Two different sets of Indian Chiefs had made their way through the crowd as their flag boys made a path for them. One Chief adorned in a neon orange feathered costume, pranced around as if he were the most beautiful peacock to ever allow someone to see him, posing with his chest out proudly as if he was saying, "Look at me." The other Chief covered in a bright royal blue feathered costume opened his arms wide to reveal an array of rainbow colored feathers perfectly lining the inside of his suit , resembling an Amazon Macaw, the colors were simply astounding. The two Indian Chiefs danced around each other as the crowd just cheered watching the two dance and bounce like magnificent creatures across the grass. After their dance was complete the two Chiefs met face to face, bowed and hugged one another in a tight embrace. Just like the performance began with the flag boys making a loud announcement of their Chiefs, they ended the same way,

"Hey now Big Chief is so pretty! My Chief! Yo Chief, is so pretty!"

The audience cheered and clapped as the two Indian groups disappeared into the large crowd.

Khori was standing in line at the snowball stand with the rest of his cousins when he seen that unsettling site of Garu and his clique walking thru the fair.

"Damn I can't get away from this nigga", mumbled Khori.

"What you say?", asked Ronnisha.

Khori just brushed her question off and asked her what flavor snowball she wanted. As he started to pay for all the snowballs Devin stopped him,

"Dang cuz, you balling like that? I could have put in on it, here" as he handed him 20 dollars on the order.

When Devin looked in his cousin's eyes he noticed he looked pale in the face,

"Dude what's up with you, you good?"

Khori nodded yes and began to walk in the opposite direction of Garu, while still keeping him in sight at all times. Ronnisha quickly kept up with her big brother,

"Where you going? The pony ride is the other way. Remember Shantee and Lenelle wanted to ride the ponies?"

Khori turned around to hand Ronnisha some money to take his little sisters on a pony ride and right at that moment he made eye contact with Garu. The connection was just a few seconds but it felt so much longer to Khori as he attempted to avoid any further contact with Garu. Khori immediately turned around and headed toward his car in the parking lot.

"Dude where are you going?", screamed Ronnisha as she watched her brother briskly walk off.

Quickly cutting thru the crowd of people Khori was almost to the parking lot when he seen two of Garu's guys standing waiting for him,

"Going somewhere Kush?"

He turned around to head back but Garu and the rest of his group was coming up with guns drawn. In that split second Khori could see that Ronnisha was following behind him as she's always done but this time had no clue as to what was going on and the amount of danger she was in at the present.

"What's up with you", asked Ronnisha.

A cluster of loud pops and bangs filled the air, like New Year's fireworks, as multiple bullets raced pass Khori, all the time diving to protect his sister from the onslaught of gunfire. The crowd scattered for safety from the goons, as Garu and his crew targeted a row of dumpsters that Khori hid behind as he hovered over Ronnisha blanketing her from any oncoming bullets. The deafening sounds of the barrage of bullets hitting the dumpsters echoed right along with the sounds of a few ricocheting off the concrete. The curtain of fire ceased, the sound of police sirens could be heard in the distance and the sound of hurrying footsteps rushed away from the scene. Khori realized he had survived Garu's attack and stood up to help Ronnisha off the ground but the site of his blood soaked shirt had him wondering where he was shot. He didn't feel any pain and didn't see any wounds but when he looked down at his sister he knew the worst has happened. Khori looked down at a lifeless Ronnisha, eyes still open, with a small hole under her left eye and her head was resting in a pool of her own blood,

"No no no no", cried out a stricken Khori.

He knew his sister was gone and the bullet her innocent body received was meant for him instead. Khori sat there, feeling as if his heart was just torn from his chest, holding his sister in his arms silently crying as four NOPD cars all came to a complete stop near the dumpsters where he was. Khori sat there quiet and motionless,

"C'mon son, let me help you", stated one police officer as he could see the catastrophe of the work of Garu laying in Khori's lap.

Khori held onto Ronnisha a little longer and slowly released his hold as the officer helped him up off the ground. The officer escorted Khori to his patrol car as another officer glanced over the horrific scene of the riddled dumpsters and Ronnisha's perished soul. Khori just sat there in total shock as the officers looked at the casings scattered over the ground, laying down markers to count off the amount of bullets fired. One officer could hear a phone ringing close by Ronnisha's body, as he reached down he could see the cracked screen of her phone read "Mommy Dearest". Khori's cell began to ring but it was Kareem on the other end, he really didn't want to answer the call because he knew what he had to say. He handed his phone to the near by officer,

"Please answer this. I can't tell them. I just can't."

The officer could see the hurt in Khori's eyes and knew the person on the other end had to be close to him, the deceased girl or both.

"I got you young man. I got you", replied the officer as he took the phone from Khori.

The officer answered the phone,

"Hello…no this is Officer Kelly. I'm here with Khori but he's a little upset right now. Can you meet me? I'm right on the side of the church in front of the parking lot on Caffin Avenue by the dumpsters…yes, he's fine."

Officer Kelly turned to Khori, handed him back his phone and let him know that his uncle was on his way. The other police officer immediately retrieved a large white sheet along with some caution tape from his squad car to cover-up Ronnisha's body and corner off the crime scene before anyone else arrives. The alert of an ambulance siren could be heard coming quickly up the street as Khori sat on the curb with his head planted in his blood stained hands. Kareem, Yolanda and Shalay came running to the side of the church searching for Khori as Officer Kelly confronted them to a halt,

"Hey, hey. Are you the gentleman I talked to on the phone? I'm Officer Kelly, Khori's right over there but I have a question for you. Were you looking for someone else also?"

"Yes! My daughter Ronnisha", replied Shalay,

"Is she here too? Is she ok?" Shalay could see the facial expression on Officer Kelly and it wasn't good at all,

"Where's my baby? Where is she? Please please sir where is my child?"

Kareem turned around, seen the large white sheet and instantly knew his niece was under there. Yolanda saw the tears begin to fall from Kareem's eyes and went straight to Shalay to console her because she hadn't seen the horrific image yet. Shalay cried out,

"Yolanda stop. I need them to find my baby. I need to find my baby."

Officer Kelly tried to comfort Shalay as he seen the pain in her face spoke to her in the calmest voice he could muster,

"Come here baby. I need you to calm down and describe to me how your daughter looks. Maybe I can get one of the other officers to check on her."

Shalay's voice shivered as she began describing Ronnisha to Officer Kelly,

"She's 16, about 5 foot 7, light brown tone, slim, she had on a green top and some dark green shorts."

Officer Kelly looked over to his partner for confirmation and the other officer put his head down in despair confirming that Shalay described the person he was looking at. Shalay then knew her worse fear just came to a culmination,

"That's not my baby over there! No! I refuse to accept that! No, no, no not my baby! Please tell me that's not my little girl over there! Please sir."

Shalay collapsed as her knees just seem to fall from under her and Officer Kelly tried to hold her up. Seeing the devastation overcome his mother, the sadness Khori was feeling was leaving his body and anger started to settle its ugly head deep in his heart. Khori stood up and began walking toward his car where he knew he had a fully loaded gun and two reserved clips but Kareem seen his nephew was headed to do something he would regret,

"Khori! Stop! Where are you going?"

Tears still flowing from his eyes Khori stopped and stood next to his car,

"Unk I gotta go. I gotta fix this shit. Them bitches killed my sister."

"You know who did this?", asked Kareem,

"If you do tell the cops."

Khori felt he couldn't talk to the police about what had happened and just clammed up to Kareem's questions. Kareem stood there stuck between trying to talk his nephew into telling the police what truly happened and wanting to help Yolanda contain Shalay's uncontrollable agony as she watched the coroners load her daughter's body into the Orleans Parish

Coroner's van. Khori was stationed firmly next to his car as Officer Kelly walked over to try and find out what exactly happened,

"So Khori what can you tell me about what took place here?"

"Me and my sister were going to my car and these guys showed up, I never seen them before and when I seen them pull out guns I pushed my sister behind the dumpster. After they stopped shooting, I seen that she was shot. They shot my sister in the face. They shot her in the face!", replied Khori.

Officer Kelly knew he wouldn't get anything else from Khori as he could see the anguish and anger in his eyes.

"I'm a let you go with your family right now but let me get some information from you, just in case we have more questions for you. Can you describe what any of the guys look like? Any markings? A tattoo? Anything?", stated Officer Kelly as he wrote down Khori's driver's license info.

CHAPTER 4

Denise was laying down on a soft blanket in the grass watching Jamal chase their daughter Ashley up the levee at the lake when she seen Jamal's nephew walk up,

"Hey Garu, you made your way over here after all. How you been boy?"

Garu sat down next to Denise,

"I'm good, I see lil Ash having some fun with Uncle Jay."

Denise asked Garu how he get to the lake because she didn't see him drive up in a car. Garu let her know that he had his friends drop him off after they left the church fair. Denise had no idea what took place at the fair and Garu didn't give any aspect that anything happened out of the ordinary.

"Boy wha cha doing here? I thought you was at that fair you told me about", asked Jamal as he walked up with Ashley straddling his foot as if she was on a carnival ride.

"I didn't wanna go to the fair anyways, it was boring, so I had my friends drop me off over here", replied Garu while picking up Ashley as he kissed her on her chubby cheeks.

Jamal reached in his cooler and handed Garu a bottle of beer,

"Well ya here now. Chill out and enjoy the sunshine neph."

Garu started playing with Ashley as she ran around the three of them in circles. Denise watched her daughter enjoy herself with her big cousin, just like other groups of people were doing at the lake with their barbecue pits smoking, music playing and a few teen boys playing ball showing off their athletic prowess for the teenage girls watching. It was a chance to just relax and enjoy the moment but Denise had no idea of the pain her former family was going through because of the actions of the man that was standing right in front of her. It started getting late and Jamal started packing up everything to get ready to leave,

"You want me to drop you off by ya moms nephew?"

"Yeah, I'm a chill over there. I don't have to head back to school til Wednesday", responded Garu as he walked with Ashley to the car.

Cedric was in the car with his family, following Kareem to Shalay's house and the car was eerily quiet as no one had any words for what just took place. Sherell sat in the passenger seat holding onto Cedric's hand for dear life as if she was scared to lose him. Tears continuously rolled down her face dripping on her shirt. Sherell couldn't believe the little girl she has known since she was Tre's age now, watched grow into a beautiful and smart young lady is gone. She tried to hide her sorrow from her little one but even at such a young age Tre could tell something is wrong and cried to get his mother's attention.

"It's ok baby, calm down. We're almost there", replied Sherell as she reached in the back of the car to comfort her almost 2 year old.

Tre continued to cry and even got louder when Lamaj tried to sooth him but at that point Sherell had her fill of his little out burst,

"Cedric Daniels, The Third I said calm down! Now that is enough! Mommy said she's gonna get you. Now stop it and fix ya face!"

Tre instantly stopped crying, wiped his eyes and finished off sniffling while he sat back in his car seat. Cedric parked behind Kareem in front of Shalay's house and watched his sister walk up to her front door like a zombie, no facial expression at all. He couldn't bring himself to get out of the car when Sherell and the kids got out and headed to the house with Yolanda. Kareem stood in the driveway waiting for his brother. He walked up to the passenger side of Cedric's car, sat down and the two brothers just sat there silent trying to be strong for each other.

"Devin said Alonna and Steven on their way. I think Khori knows who shot at him but he's either scared to say or he's thinking of doing something stupid", stated Kareem as he pulled out a pack of cigarettes out of his pocket.

"We gotta find out before he does something he's gonna regret later", replied Cedric.

Kareem started looking in his phone,

"I'm already ahead of you. I texted Levi on my way here. I'm just waiting on him to text me back."

Levi was an old neighborhood friend of the brothers that had deep connections in the criminal world of the city. Anything underground, underhanded or undesirable going on in New Orleans, Levi had a hand in it or knew someone that did. He was the best option for Kareem to find out any information on what really went down with Khori, besides his connection with the family goes deep.

    Devin and Khori sat in Alonna's backyard trying to wrap their head around what happened at the fair, Devin trying to figure out why someone would shoot at his cousins and Khori trying to figure out how to kill Garu.

Devin could see his cousin wasn't heartbroken like he was but was more angered than anything,

"Dude, you have no idea who did this or do you? Cause I'm not above from helping you get them for what they did Nisha, for real."

Khori looked at his cousin and wanted to tell him but knew it was a bad idea, Devin was not mentally or morally ready for what Khori had in mind. He just responded in a calming voice,

"No cuz, I couldn't tell you who they were. It happened so fast that I couldn't get a look at any of their faces."

Khori asked Devin for a shirt so he could change and take a shower cause he still had on the shirt with Ronnisha's blood all over it. They went inside to Semaj sitting on the sofa in a daze, Dashanae laying sleep with Lenelle and Shantee close to her and Zachariah was just sitting in the kitchen with his head down on the kitchen table. Khori got in the shower and let the hot water just run down his face thinking of a way to get rid of Garu for good without it coming back to him. He started running scenarios thru his mind of how he could ambush Garu but that wouldn't work because he always has an entourage surrounding him. Then he thought about taking Garu's members out one at a time but that would alert Garu and he would go into hiding, so that wouldn't work either. Khori's college studies of plants then came to mind and he finally came up with a plan but it would to take some serious finesse to accomplish. When Khori was getting dressed he seen he had missed a call but whoever it was left a voice message,

"Hello, this message is for Khori Daniels, my name is Detective Jason Babineaux. Officer James Kelly gave me your number and I have a few questions for you. Please give me a call as soon as you get this."

Khori really didn't want to talk to anymore police officers but to keep them from searching any deeper he felt he had to cooperate with them, so he called the number back. Detective Babineaux quickly answered and informed Khori that they had video of the incident from a nearby corner grocery store surveillance camera but the video wasn't clear enough to make out any faces. He also told him that because of all the vehicles that sped off during the shooting it will take some time trying to figure out if any of the cars were apart of the crime. In one way Khori was upset that they weren't able to identify Garu and his followers but in another way he was content that they couldn't because that meant he would be able to extract his revenge on the whole lot. Detective Babineaux let Khori know he would be keeping in touch with him and his mother with any information he finds and if he could remember anything about the event to give him a call. Khori ended the call and immediately started planning his raged vengeance on Garu and everyone involved with Ronnisha's death.

Delores sat on the end of her bed with not a tear left to cry, eyes swollen and her heart completely shattered at the fact that one of her grandchildren is no longer with her. She felt like it was her fault because she insisted that all of her grandkids be at the church today. Delores felt like her insides were balling up in knots at the idea that if she didn't persist with her children to bring everyone to church that Ronnisha would still be with them. She desperately wanted to call her daughter but couldn't remember Shalay's number for some reason, at that moment she heard the doorbell ring. When Delores got to the front door she seen it was Steven,

"Baby what are you doing here? I thought you and Alonna was going by Shalay."

Steven told Delores they all were going there together and that he felt Shalay really needs her mother with her at this time. Delores gladly grabbed her purse and headed out with them,

"Baby I wanted to go but I didn't want to bother her."

"Mama that's nonsense, we're all family and right now we need each other more than ever", replied Steven as he walked Delores to the car. Alonna was sitting in the backseat, eyes bloodshot red and tears flowing like the Mississippi River. Delores reached back, held onto her daughter's hand and the energy Alonna felt just from her mother's touch was enough to strengthen her,

"Baby, The Lord got us through a lot of things and He will get us through this too. I know it hurts baby, trust me I do but we will be ok. I have faith in The Almighty and I have faith in the strength of this family. We will see brighter days."

Alonna just cried in the backseat hoping this nightmare would end,

"Mama, I don't understand how somebody could be that heartless and start shooting at a church function with all those people around. What kind of animal does such a thing? Ronnisha had her whole life ahead of her, she was just getting started."

Steven tried to hold back the tears but the thought of not seeing his happy and always smiling niece's face rocked him,

"Baby whoever it was will get what's coming to him, Ronnisha will get justice."

Cedric was still standing outside when he seen Kevin pull up to Shalay's house, he still hadn't made it inside yet.

"Ced, you ok bro? Where's Shay?", asked Kevin as he quickly walked up.

Cedric let his friend know that she was inside with everybody else and that he's waiting on Alonna to show up. When Kevin got inside he seen Yolanda and Sherell sitting next to Shalay on the sofa holding Tre on her lap as he fell asleep in her embrace. Kevin fell to his knees in front of Shalay's feet, "Baby I am so sorry" and laid his head on her knee. Shalay reached out and her fingers slid thru Kevin's dark brown colored hair as she held onto his head,

"Thank you for coming Kev."

Kareem went to pick up Tre from Shalay's lap,

"Leave my baby here, he's sleeping. I'm fine."

Everybody in the house knew that statement wasn't true, Shalay wasn't doing well and the persona that she is was just about to wear off as her mother walked in the door. Shalay looked up at her mother's worried face and instantly fell apart. She handed her sleeping nephew to Sherell and ran to Delores' arms,

"Mommy my baby is gone. They killed my baby. She didn't do anybody anything. She was a good girl. Why did they have to do her like that? My baby."

Delores just held onto her daughter trying to comfort her as best as she can. Cedric finally made his way inside, seen his mother holding on to his sister and couldn't hold back the tears any longer. The agony he seen his sister going through hurt him to his very being as he went to Kareem,

"You heard anything from Levi yet?"

Kareem let him know Levi texted him back a few minutes ago and that he'll let him know as soon as he gets any kind of information.

"Whoever this bitch is he gotta pay for what he did", replied Cedric.

"The bitch paying with his life", responded Kareem.

Cedric knew exactly what his little brother meant by that and was comfortable with knowing Levi would be able to complete the job for them,

"Tell him this has to be discreet. No off the wall crazy shit. When he finds out who's responsible for this, make it look like a simple missing person incident."

Kareem nodded his head and understood what his brother was talking about. Levi's "hits" usually were out in the open assaults with the victims displayed dead in broad daylight but in a case like this the brothers didn't want any of that, they just wanted the person gone for good. The brothers knew they couldn't let any of their family members know what they were planning because it would get turned down abruptly by everyone. But seeing the hurt that blanketed the entire family over Ronnisha's death they knew they had to do something because they didn't think the police would be able to.

Everybody was in the den while Lamaj sat on the floor in Ronnisha's room just looking at how she left it, he could still smell her presence. All kinds of emotions rain thru Lamaj as he sat there thinking about his cousin because they were the same age and knowing of all her plans after high school. Ronnisha had two unfinished artwork projects still sitting on easels with her paint brushes close by, pictures of French Quarter cafes and pictures of a line of horse carriages in front of the St. Louis Cathedral were taped to the canvases. Lamaj just sat in amazement of her talent and knew he would never get to see her finish them again. But the one thing that caught his eye was two pictures of him and Devin in their football uniforms side by side taped to Ronnisha's mirror. He started to notice a lot of pictures Ronnisha had of her family all over her room, pictures of her brothers and sisters, pictures of her cousins and all of them captured without the person knowing she had taken the photo of them. Lamaj was just hurting at the thought that he couldn't talk to her anymore, listen to her laugh at his jokes or share a simple moment together. He didn't realize how much he loved his cousin until it was too late.

CHAPTER 5

It was a rainy Wednesday morning and Khori was in his room getting ready for his drive back to school in Texas when his mother walked in,

"Son do you really have to go back so soon?"

He didn't want to leave his family but there was some things he needed to take care of before Ronnisha's funeral on Saturday,

"Mama I promise I will be back Friday night or early Saturday morning. I just need to take care of this one assignment and I'm good."

Khori grabbed his duffle bags and started putting them in the trunk of his car when the nagging feeling of his little sister always being right there next to him when he's heading back to Texas was not there anymore. It hurt something serious and that pain fueled his rage inside. He took a deep breath to get his composure cause he didn't want his mother seeing him break down as he closed the trunk and got in his car to head out. Shalay walked up to his window,

"Please drive safe baby. I'll see you when you get back"

then kissed him on the forehead as she has ever since he was a toddler. Khori headed to the Interstate with one thing on his mind and one thing only, destroying Garu and everyone that had anything to do with his little sister's death. He knew he had to try to do it alone because he didn't want to involve anyone else but he also needed an alibi just in case any questions got asked. Khori called Devin,

"What up cuz, I'm heading back to Texas but I'm a be back Friday night. But I'm a need a big favor from you."

"Anything fam", replied Devin.

Khori then told Devin if anyone ask him that he and Khori came back to New Orleans together. Devin didn't even ask why and agreed to help his cousin,

"You just heading back to school? I left first thing this morning, I just had to get out the city."

Khori understood where his cousin was coming from and had the same feelings toward being in New Orleans at the time but he knew all the items he needed to accomplish his goals were in his dorm room. He made his way down the long Interstate as he passed thru Beaumont, Khori knew he only had a few more hours before he was in College Station and he could get started on his project. He knew he wouldn't have any problems once he got to school, being one of the top student botanist in his class, doing independent projects are normal to see from him and it wouldn't cause any alarms. He had a plan to use his botanical studies to eliminate his foes in one clean sweep, he just needed to get to the school's Horticultural Science Center and then his lab which was hidden at his dorm on the roof where he had his own personal greenhouse.

The thing Khori's family didn't know about him was that he is not only in the top five of student botanist at Texas A&M but he also has the title of "The Weed Man" known as Kush on campus. Khori created a strain of marijuana that is so potent that students flock to him to get a sample of what he calls "The Hulk 2.0" because of its bright green buds and purple stems. Khori became a target for Garu because he sells his product cheaper than Garu's regular weed and because he grows his own plants, Khori is never low on supply. Garu always tried to find where Khori hides his inventory but always came up short, only finding small baggies at the most. Khori made sure to keep his secret from everyone on campus except for the maintenance man Mr. Jay that's over the dormitories on campus, he and Khori are the only ones with a key to the roof of his dorm. Khori keeps Mr. Jay supplied with free marijuana for his wife who has epilepsy and Mr. Jay keeps Khori's greenhouse and lab a secret from everyone else, the arrangement was perfect. Khori had made it to the school's Horticultural Science Center's greenhouse where he knew they had several castor oil plants because he needed as many seeds as he could get his hands on. After conversing with a few students he knew in the nursery, Khori began cultivating as many castor oil plant seeds he could without messing up the plants normal process in growing. He made a beeline straight to his little lab where his project would take form. See many people know castor oil plants to produce exactly what it says, castor oil which is used for so many purposes. But Khori also knew that with the right process the seeds could be used to produce ricin which is highly poisonous to humans and virtually untraceable. Khori sat and studied like he was getting ready for a final exam but this test had a different outcome, either he pass or he fail. He knew he didn't want the latter so he paid close attention to his levels, his temps and his mixtures to make sure everything was perfect.

   Kareem was getting dressed to head out to open up the shop like he does every morning when he seen a text from Levi,

"I got some info and we need to be face to face".

Kareem called Levi and just said,

"Meet me at the shop on Broad in 20" and ended the call.

He was making his way to the shop when he called Cedric,

"Big bro, Levi said he has some information for us. He's meeting up with me at the shop in a few."

Cedric was already at work and couldn't leave,

"I'm a pass over as soon as I get off today."

When Kareem pulled up to his barber shop Levi was already parked waiting on him,

"What's good Reem."

Kareem was anxious to hear what Levi had to say and rushed inside,

"Chilling homie chilling, what you got for me?"

Levi started telling Kareem about his home girl Leslie who heard this young guy talk about how he had a shootout at a church and she told him where to find the guy. Levi ran into him at a "hole in the wall" bar room Uptown on Jackson Ave and got him drunk,

"You know niggas talk when they drunk. A drunk soul speaks a sober mind."

Kareem really wasn't in the mood for story time and needed Levi to hurry up before any of his clients or staff walk in the shop,

"Ok bruh, so what did he have to say? What or who was involved in the shooting?"

Levi then told Kareem what the drunk told him, that the shooting was between two rival dealers, Garu and Kush. Kareem was confused because he didn't know how his nephew or niece would be involved in a rival between two dealers. Kareem was lost for words when Levi told him Kush's real name,

"Dog that can't be true. My nephew is one of those cool nerds in college. You telling me Khori is a dealer? No."

Levi told him that Khori started out selling Garu a few years ago and that's what created the rival but it only escalated to a few physical altercations, nothing too serious that campus police couldn't handle.

"Wait they go to school together?", asked Kareem.

Levi just nodded his head yes as he went on about how the guy didn't know they killed a girl until they seen it on the news, they thought they shot Kush and that Garu been laying low with his crew for a few days now at one of his trap houses in the East. Kareem didn't know how to take the information that Levi just gave him but one thing definitely he was pissed,

"I can't believe this boy knew who shot his sister and instead of telling them he ain't say one damn word to the police about it. The fuck wrong with him."

"C'mon now Reem, if that boy tell them it was over two dope dealers and he's one of them. He going straight to jail and you know this", replied Levi.

Kareem knew Levi was telling the truth but was upset that his nephew kept that away from him. Levi informed Kareem that he is going to find Garu no matter what,

"She was never in that life homie, baby girl had too much going for her."

Kareem went to his safe in his office, pulled out two stacks of 50 dollar bills and handed it to Levi,

"I need this done by Saturday. When I lay Ronnisha to rest I need to know Garu is in the ground. But this has to be discreet, understood."

"Say homie, I don't need ya money for this one. That dude as good as gone, ya heard me. You know what this is", replied Levi.

Kareem stuffed the money in an envelope and put it directly in Levi's hand,

"I know homie."

As Levi was leaving the shop Yolanda was walking in,

"Hey Levi. How you been boy?"

Levi gave Yolanda a hug and kiss on the cheek,

"I'm good Queen, real good" as he headed to the exit door.

Yolanda watched Levi get in his truck, drive off and knew Levi wasn't at the shop for a hair cut but she was afraid to ask Kareem because she knows what Levi specializes in. She just sat in her man's office, watched as she could see Kareem's mind was elsewhere and knew it couldn't be anything good.

Khori woke up in his lab after a long day of prepping to the sun peeking thru a small window and looked over to a table that had a mason jar half full with a white powdery substance. He knew he had successfully produced his ricin and now its time to test it to make sure it actually works. Khori collected a teaspoon amount in a small baggy and headed to the university's Veterinary Division of Research where he knew they housed a large quantity of lab rats and mice. As he made his way through the dorm to get to his car he ran into a classmate that heard about his sister's untimely death,

"Dude I'm so sorry for your loss."

Khori thought to himself,

"Man you didn't even know my sister. Why you sorry for my loss?" but instead of saying that out loud he just nodded yes and continued out the door to the parking lot.

When he started his engine, he looked up to see a female classmate walking up to his car and Khori whispered to himself,

"Not another one. I can't do this fake feeling sorry for me shit all day."

"Hey Kush, I seen you when you came in but you disappeared on me. I wanted to chill with you last night", stated the young lady as she leaned in Khori's passenger side window.

Khori put on a phony smile,

"Erica, you trying to get some of this dick. You know you never wanted to chill with me before."

Erica laughed,

"Boy, stop playing with me. Hit me up when you get back from wherever you going", as she walked off.

Khori smiled and pulled off knowing he's going to call Erica as soon as he gets back to his dorm room. Erica has always been a tease for Khori with her athletic frame, gorgeous lips, big brown eyes and adorable dimples that you could pour a cup of water in. He felt she was the ultimate teaser, always soft kisses on the cheek like you would do a baby, at house parties she would grind on him like a Jamaican dancehall star and leave it only to just that, dancing. Erica knew Khori really liked her but she kept him in the friend zone and that drove him crazy.

Devin was sitting on a bench in the weight room when his coach walked up to him,

"Hey son, you good? I heard the news and I'm so sorry about your cousin."

"I'm good Coach Howard. It just bothers me that somebody gunned her down like that, she wasn't apart of that lifestyle and they almost took out my other cousin Khori, he was with her", replied Devin.

Coach Howard could see that Devin's mind wasn't focused on anything in the weight room and suggested that he go to clear it,

"I know the pain you're going through, loss a brother in a senseless shooting when I was a teen. But I promise it gets better son. You just need to focus on close friends, family and remember the good times."

Devin shook his head no,

"No offense coach but I just need to hit these weights and get ready for the season."

Coach Howard knew one of his key players was nowhere near focused or ready for any type of workout,

"Go see Marcus and tell him that I said bring you by Kush."

Marcus was the number one corner-back on the team, let alone considered the number one corner-back in the Southeastern Conference (SEC) and Coach Howard knew he was an avid smoker. Devin listened to his coach and found Marcus on the treadmill doing his normal high speed training,

"Hey dude, coach said you know how to get in touch with Kush."

Marcus laughed as he stopped the treadmill,

"You wanna smoke? Not the prodigal son. Welcome to the dark side my nigga."

"Man stop it. I just need to get my head straight. Got a lot on my mind", replied Devin.

Marcus knew about Ronnisha, stopped smiling and hugged Devin,

"I got you bro. Let me hit the showers real quick and we can head out. Kush lives on campus so he's close."

Devin heard about Kush and Garu but didn't associate himself with either of the two. He knew Marcus and a few other players partake in smoking but felt it hinders their performance on the field,

"Dude how you smoke and perform on the field like you do?"

"Man I only blaze on our off days. Never before practice or a game, strictly recreation my nigga. Coach be on me about it but as long as I'm a shut down corner, he really can't say too much. Shit I stay clean for those surprise piss test", replied Marcus.

The two headed out as Marcus texted Kush to meet up with him.

Khori walked in the research center, scanned the lobby, saw several security cameras positioned in every corner of the lobby and quickly put his head down to avoid having his face seen. He knew he would need a way to get pass the security doors that led to the storage areas where the small animals were held. He seen a few students walk in a near by locker room with their white coats on but walk out without them and right then he knew he needed to get in one of those lockers. Right as he was walking to the locker room he received a text,

"My buddy wants to see your Hulk collection."

Khori knew he had a customer in route to his dorm just from the text.

"Bet, give me a few.", replied Khori.

He walked up to a locker, pulled on the handle and was surprised that it was unlocked. Khori put on the lab coat, clipped on the student badge and casually walked to the double doors where the sign "Laboratory/Biomedical Research" was over it. He followed more signs in the hallway that directed him straight to the very place he wanted to be. Khori walked up to the door where the lab rats were kept, scanned the student ID card he had and the door popped right open. He walked in and instantly started looking for security cameras in the room but seen none. He knew he was safe to do what he had come to do but knew he had to move fast because there were students all over the research area. Khori put on some latex gloves he seen on the table, put on a medical mask, carefully took the small baggy he had tucked away in his pocket and went to pick up one of the white rats that was in a cage with a few others. He made sure to open the baggy slowly to not spill any of it, he then put the rat's nose in the small baggy, sprinkled a little of the white powder on the back of the animal and then carefully placed him back in the cage with all the other rats. Khori felt bad that he was poisoning the animal but he had to make sure his concoction was correct,

"Sorry little buddy."

He set the stopwatch on his phone to count down how long it would take to see some sort of reaction from the powder on the rodent. The white rat began walking thru the colony of other rats, drinking from the water container like normal and two minutes went by with no sign of distress from the little white victim, Khori thought he had failed. But right at three minutes Khori saw several rats start to chase their tails, running in circles and roll over on their backs as their bodies slowly stopped moving. Eventually all 22 critters were laying on their backs deceased and Khori knew he had created a very potent batch of ricin. He then got a large black garbage bag, placed every one of the dead rodents in it and sprayed the cage down with water because he didn't want any of the students to accidentally touch any left over residue from the poison.

Devin and Marcus were parked in front of one of the student dorms when Devin realized it was Khori's dorm,

"My cousin stays in this dorm."

"I didn't know you had a cousin that went here too", replied Marcus.

Devin told Marcus they travel in different groups and that not too many people know they are related but they always hang together when they are home.

"I don't wanna be sitting here waiting all day for some reggie, where this dude at?", asked Devin.

Marcus laughed,

"Hulk 2.0 is far from reggie. Dude cool as hell but is like a science geek, grows his own high quality shit and keeps a large supply. That's why him and Garu always beefing cause he putting him outta business."

Devin knew Garu was a small time dealer on campus and was from his hometown but never tried or wanted to associate himself with Garu because of it. He now wondered if he ever seen this Kush character Marcus keeps talking about so vividly,

"So I guess Garu got it out for Ole boy then?"

"They may have had a few scuffles but nothing too drastic because campus police always close around. Garu is a grimy nigga but he don't want no smoke. Kush ain't the one to play with and will draw down on you quick", replied Marcus as he got a text from Kush stating he's pulling up now.

Devin sat patiently on the steps in front of the dorm when he seen his cousin Khori pull up and park. The two cousins seen each other and got really nervous. Devin because he didn't want his cousin knowing he was there to buy weed and Khori because he didn't want his cousin to know he's about to sell some weed. Marcus did more than break the ice when Khori got out of his car, he shattered it with three simple words,

"My nigga Kush!"

Devin face showed every bit of shock and surprise when he heard that,

"You Kush? Really bruh, you Kush?"

Marcus looked confused because he could tell they knew each other just from how they were looking at one another,

"I'm guessing y'all know each other then. Well since all the introduction is over with, I'm a need a 10 piece."

Khori put his head down as he walked to the dumpster and threw a large black garbage bag in it,

"I got you dude but how out of everybody on campus you bring my cousin over here."

Marcus looked perplexed as he turned to Devin smiling and nodding his head yes,

"Yup that's the cousin I was telling you about."

CHAPTER 6

Kareem and Cedric went to their mother's house together because she said she had something important to talk to them about. As they walked up to the house they seen their mother fiddling in her flower bed like she does every once in awhile,

"Hey boys, what y'all doing here?", asked Delores.

"Mama you called us to come over here", replied Kareem.

Delores looked a little confused at first,

"I did? Oh yeah! I needed y'all to do something for me but I don't need either of your sisters to know about it."

Cedric wondered what was so secretive his mother wanted them to do,

"Mama, we not going kill Mrs. Evans little dog for you."

Delores giggled,

"Boy stop playing with me. Besides, I got a BB gun for his lil ass when he comes in my yard shitting again", as she looked over her shoulder at her next door neighbor's house.

Delores then told her sons that she needs them to go to the funeral home and pay for Ronnisha's service,

"I know Shalay is going through a very hard time and I don't want her worrying about how she's going to pay for any of this. She's a headstrong woman that will do without before asking for help, so take this envelope and tell Nathan Bordelon I said this should take care of everything we discussed."

Kareem replied,

"Mama, you don't need to do this, Shalay probably got it all covered."

Delores gave Kareem that strong mother's look that every child received once or twice in their lives when they misbehave,

"Yes ma'am, I'm a go take care of that right now."

Cedric laughed out loud hard,

"You got anything else you wanna say Reem?"

Kareem took the envelope from his mother and started walking to his car when Delores had another statement for him,

"Son, I was told Levi been at your shop. Now you know that boy ain't nothing but trouble, he been a bad seed since he was little and I don't wanna hear about you doing any funny business with him."

"Mama, I'm good. He was just passing thru", replied Kareem.

Delores' boys got in the car and headed to the funeral home as she requested.

"Yolanda talk too much man. She seen Levi leave the shop after he told me about Garu. She asked me why he was there and I told her don't worry about it", stated Kareem.

"Bro she just concerned cause she knows what Levi bout, that's all. As long as she doesn't know about our situation we good. She doesn't know right?", replied Cedric.

Kareem looked at his brother sarcastically,

"What you take me for, Boo Boo The Fool? Hell no!"

Cedric told Kareem he needed to take care of some very important paperwork and could he drop him off to his car. Kareem complied and went on alone to run the errand his mother set out for him.

Devin and Khori were sitting on the balcony at Khori's dorm room smoking when Devin asked a question that been bothering him for awhile,

"Cuz, did Garu have anything to do with Ronnisha? Cause from what I'm hearing y'all got a big beef going on."

The silence on the balcony was deafening and Devin automatically knew his cousin knew who shot at him that day. Devin looked Khori in the eye this time when he asked,

"How could you just be quiet while the person responsible for your own sister's death walk around free?"

"I'm taking care of it alright", replied Khori.

At this point anger is starting to creep in on Devin,

"Nigga this ain't no damn gangsta series on TV you looking at, where you walk in with a AK and spray the place to get your revenge on everybody. Nigga you should have told the damn cops who shot her!"

Khori tried to get out another word when Devin jumped up and grabbed his cousin around the neck, leaning him over the edge of the balcony,

"You should have told the damn police. You trying to play judge and jury and yo mama gone have to bury two of her kids instead of one if you fuck up."

Khori calmly looked Devin in the eyes,

"Nigga I told you I got this shit under control. Get yo fucking hands off of me before we both end up falling off this damn balcony."

Khori went inside and started packing to leave,

"Like I told you yesterday morning, we left together to head back to New Orleans if anybody asked."

Devin nodded yes and continued to smoke his blunt on the balcony. Khori smiled at Devin with a duffle bag and a suitcase in hand while standing at his front door,

"Cuz the next time you put yo hands on me I'm a knock yo big ass out. Strong ass muthafucka."

Khori opened the door to leave and there stood Erica that was just about to knock,

"So you gone leave me again and not even call this time."

Khori was stuck trying to explain to Erica how he forgot that they were suppose to hang out today but his cousin came to his rescue,

"It's my fault Erica. I came over by my cuz and we got to talking and the time just got away from us."

"Hey Devin, I didn't know Kush was your cousin", responded Erica.

Khori was relieved that Devin came up with a quick explanation but asked,

"How y'all know each other?"

"Duh, star football player everybody knows Devin besides he's in like two of my classes. But the real question is where are you running off to this time", replied Erica.

Khori told her he had to get back to New Orleans for his sister's service and he had an idea to use Erica as an alibi,

"You can come along for the ride if you want to."

Erica agreed and told Khori she needs a few minutes to gather a few of her things for the trip,

"I need to get away anyways and I need to keep you outta trouble."

Khori went to go bring his things to his car and told Devin to lock up when he leaves.

"You sure you want her coming with you cuz", asked Devin.

Khori smiled as he whispered,

"Alibis come in all forms fam."

The two cousins hugged it out and Khori went on his way as Erica rushed to get her things for the road trip.

Kevin Talport went over to check on Shalay during lunch like he has everyday since that awful Sunday afternoon. When he knocked on the door he found Shalay coming from the side of the house with some gardening gloves on and a small garden shovel,

"Hey babygirl, what you doing?"

"Hey Kev, I gotta get these weeds up out this flower bed. Delores would kick my ass if she seen how bad I let this get. What you doing here? You keep coming around and I'm a start thinking you crushing on me", responded Shalay.

Kevin smiled as he watched her work her garden,

"Maybe I am."

Shalay looked up at Kevin standing next to her,

"Yeah ok, sweaty and covered in dirt. That's a big turn on. Stop playing with me white boy."

Kevin sat down on the porch bench as he watched Shalay pick and pull at unwanted sprouts in her flower bed. They stayed outside for a few minutes as Shalay gathered up her utensils,

"Ok let me get back inside and cleaned up cause I did as much as I'm a do today."

They walked inside,

"Kev go fix us something to drink. A cold iced tea sounds real good right about now unless you wanna come help me wash my back", laughed Shalay as she went in her bedroom.

"I'll be right there. Don't start without me", replied Kevin.

Shalay started her shower, laid out some clothes to put on and went in the bathroom to clean up. Shalay stood in the shower just letting the hot water run down her face and body, her tears easily mixing in with the water as the pain of losing her daughter continued to stab at her heart. She tries to keep a strong demeanor in front of people and times like this allows her to let out all her torment. Shalay slowly sat down in the shower with her knees in her chest holding onto her lower legs heard Kevin call for her,

"You ok in there baby? You need some help in there?"

"I'm fine. I'm about to come out in a second", responded Shalay as she pulled herself together.

She quickly washed herself, got out the shower to dry off and walked in her bedroom with a towel wrapped around herself to Kevin sitting in a chair in her room with two cold glasses of iced tea. Shalay smiled,

"You a mess white boy. You was suppose to come in and wash my back. I knew you was scary."

Kevin laughed as he stood up and walked to Shalay,

"Who said I was scary? I was just waiting for you to come out all wet."

He then gave her a glass of tea, kissed her on the cheek and walked out of the bedroom to let her get dressed,

"That boy gone have me attack his sexy ass", whispered Shalay.

Cedric drove up Tchoupitoulas street dreading to have to meet with Denise but he knew he needed those papers signed. He pulled up to the converted warehouse that is now luxury lofts and took in a deep breath as he turned off his car. Cedric could see Denise was at the park across the street from her apartments playing with her daughter Ashley. She knew he was on his way to her and agreed to meet up to finish the paperwork.

Denise had a change of heart after hearing about Ronnisha and was more than willing to finalize their divorce papers. Cedric walked up to Denise sitting on a bench in front of the playground, she stood up and gave Cedric a very warm comforting hug,

"I am so sorry to hear about Ronnisha Ced. That baby did not deserve that."

Cedric thanked her for her condolences and sat down next to Denise on the bench as he watched Ashley run around playing on the monkey bars,

"She is getting big, she's three now right?"

"Yeah and eating everything in sight. Lil Cedric is two now?", asked Denise.

Cedric let her know he will be two in a month and the two began talking like two friends who haven't spoke in awhile, it was new and refreshing for the both of them. At that point Cedric didn't want to bring up the reason for his visit and Denise eased his concerns when she asked for the papers herself. As she was signing the last sheet her cell started ringing,

"Hey boy. No your uncle still at work. Ok, me and your lil buddy will be right here. Bye."

Denise ended the call, finished the last sheet and handed over all the paperwork to Cedric,

"Well I guess that's it. We are officially divorced sir."

"Thank you", replied Cedric as he slid the papers in a manila envelope.

Denise smiled and turned to Ashley,

"Ash, Garu coming to see you."

Ashley jumped up and down in excitement yelling,

"Garu Garu Garu!"

Cedric heard the name and couldn't imagine that it was the same person he and Kareem were searching for,

"Garu?"

"Oh that's Jamal's nephew and Ashley just loves to wrestle with him", replied Denise.

Cedric had one more question and the right answer would confirm his assumptions,

"He doesn't go to Texas A&M does he cause Khori knows a Garu at his school."

"He sure does, studying business management", responded Denise.

"Well let me get outta here and let you enjoy this pretty day with that pretty little girl", stated

Cedric as he started walking back to his car.

   Kevin and Shalay sat on her sofa looking at an old TV sitcom when Shalay got really comfortable with Kevin and laid her head on his shoulder while stretching her leg across his lap. Kevin just rubbed his warm hands on her back as Shalay nuzzled her face into his shoulder,

"This feels nice."

Kevin just acknowledged Shalay's statement and caressed her thigh that was sprawled across his lap as he asked,

"You ok babe?"

"Yeah, I didn't know how much I needed this until you came over", answered Shalay.

Kevin put one finger under her chin and raised her head to look her in the eyes,

"This could be all the time if you stop being scary."

He then kissed Shalay's luscious lips and pulled her closer to him but Shalay pushed away,

"Kev, what are you doing? I can't."

Kevin then expressed to Shalay,

"But I can, baby I have been feeling you for a very long time but you haven't been catching any of my attempts. I just wanna be part of you. I wanna be more than just your business partner. I wanna be more than your friend. I wanna be more than your crazy white boy. I wanna be there for you when you don't need me to, cause you are everything I need."

Shalay got up and mounted herself on Kevin's lap as she looked into his honest speaking eyes,

"White boy, you are crazy. Where did all this come from?"

"It been here, I just got the courage to tell you", replied Kevin.

The two started erotically kissing one another as Kevin's hands slithered under Shalay's shirt up her back sending chills through her. Shalay started to pull at Kevin's shirt trying to take it off when she felt his nature rise in his pants and press against her pussy,

"Oh my goodness, somebody is awake."

She started to dry hump on the mound protruding from his pants, the friction aroused both of them and Shalay could feel herself get extremely moist the more she grinded against him. Kevin turned and laid Shalay on the sofa,

"I gotta taste it first", as he eased her pink boy shorts off exposing a plump shaved pussy.

He held her legs up and open so that he could get a perfect view of his meal,

"Damn that's pretty."

Shalay started rubbing her fat pussy lips and with one finger began stroking her throbbing clit while Kevin watched. He moved her hand, went down and started stroking her clit with his tongue. Shalay couldn't believe what was happening and the feeling she was feeling was simply amazing as Kevin's tongue flicked and fucked her soaking wet pussy. Kevin was less than three minutes in at eating her when Shalay couldn't hold on anymore and came in his mouth. He stood up to unbuckle his pants as Shalay sat up to watch him pull out his manhood and the revealing was more than she expected.

"Oh I gotta suck this muthafucka", stated Shalay as she put her hand around the base of Kevin's dick and her fingers didn't touch.

She pushed herself onto his heated muscle mass and she could feel the head of his dick press pass her throat instantly causing her to gag on it. Shalay continued to suck on him as she stroked his shaft, the whole time thinking about how good that big dick would feel filling her up. She then stopped sucking, laid herself on the floor and waited for him to come down to enter her. Kevin got down on his knees, positioned his dick head toward the opening of her and slowly inserted himself deep into her. The gasp she let out was what he needed to hear to know she was pleased with the feeling of his muscle stroking the sides of her walls. The sounds of skin slapping together and macaroni n cheese being stirred filled the room as the two fucked each other into an ecstasy filled sweaty workout.

CHAPTER 7

Cedric couldn't believe the person they been looking for was right under their nose but the only thing now was to actually get eyes on him. Cedric didn't want to sit and wait around to see if or when Garu would show up because it would cause alarm if anyone would see him just posted up at the corner in that neighborhood. He figured he would go to Jamal and get his sympathy because of Ronnisha, so he drove out to his job in Michoud. As he made his way down Interstate 10 East, Cedric remembered he and Jamal's last encounter and truly hoped they could talk to each other like men. Cedric wanted to call Kareem but didn't want Jamal to become defensive if he seen both of the brothers show up at his job. He felt it was going to be tough enough with him showing up at Jamal's job asking him questions about his nephew. As he pulled into the parking lot his adrenaline began to flow and he was anxious to get answers. Cedric walked up to the front security desk and asked,

"Excuse me sir, I don't mean to bother you but is Sgt. Jamal Green available?"

The security guard asked who's asking and after Cedric told him his name the officer got on the phone to call Jamal,

"Sgt. Green, a Mr. Daniels is here for you. Yes sir. I'll let him know."

The officer had Cedric wait in the lobby while Jamal arrived but Cedric couldn't sit down because his nerves was getting the best of him. He was so close to finding the guy who had a hand in killing his niece and waiting was not one of the options but he did just that. Jamal finally arrived with a puzzled face as he seen Cedric standing in the lobby waiting for him,

"Can I help you."

"I know I'm not someone you want to see at your place of business but I had to come talk to you because it is extremely important", replied Cedric.

Jamal became very guarded because he recalled the last conversation he and Cedric had ended in him getting up off the ground,

"Dude, what you want?"

Cedric then began to tell him about how he had information about Garu and how he was named in the murder of Ronnisha. He told him that he just wanted to talk to Garu and find out who actually shot his niece. Cedric humbled himself to try and get Jamal to help him but it all fell on deaf ears as Jamal replied,

"Look, I don't know where Garu is and I haven't talk to him in days, so you can take your info somewhere else."

"So it's like that, you not gone even try and help?", stated Cedric.

Jamal walked up to Cedric, stared him straight in his eyes with a heartless facial expression and replied in a whisper so that no one around could hear but Cedric,

"It's just like that. Now get the fuck off the property before I call the guards to escort yo ass off."

Cedric was pissed but he knew he couldn't do anything in the lobby or risk being arrested, so he turned around without saying a word and walked to his car.

Devin was in his room packing to head back to New Orleans but thinking about his cousin had him in total distress. He had to tell someone about Khori but he didn't know who, if he told his aunt Shalay it would destroy her, if he told his uncle Cedric he would probably destroy Khori and telling his mother or Steven is like telling everyone. He had only one person he knew would keep it between them and try and solve the problem, so he called his uncle Kareem. Kareem was at his shop going over his books when he received a call from Devin,

"What's good nephew? You on your way?"

"In a minute Unk. Before I get there I needed to talk to you about something", replied Devin.

Devin then told Kareem how he found out that Khori has been going by the alias "Kush" and that he and Garu been having some serious beef going on over Marijuana on campus. He told him that Garu and his crew shot at Khori that Sunday at the fair and that Khori is now on his way back to New Orleans with revenge on his mind.

"Do you know if he made it here yet?", asked Kareem.

"He left a lil over five hours ago Unk, I know I should have called you earlier but I didn't know how to tell you", answered Devin.

Kareem let him know it was ok and that he was going to get in touch with Khori.

"This boy trying to get his ass killed", mumbled Kareem as he ended the call with his concerned nephew.

Kareem was just about to call Khori when he heard one of his barbers shout out,

"What's good wit cha Ced?"

He got up from his desk to only walk into his brother as he stepped into his office,

"Nigga we gotta talk."

Kareem thinking he was talking about Khori,

"I'm a take care of it. I just gotta find that lil nigga before he do something stupid."

"Who you talking about? I'm talking about Jamal bitch ass and his nephew Garu. Yes, Garu is Jamal Green's nephew", replied Cedric.

Kareem sat back in complete shock,

"Nigga you lying. How you find that out?"

Cedric then told his brother how he was by Denise getting his divorce papers signed and how Garu called her. He then told Kareem how he tried to talk to Jamal so that he could talk to Garu and how Jamal told him in so many words to "go fuck off". Kareem then stated the obvious to Cedric,

"Dude this muthafucka was fucking yo wife behind yo back, got into a straight fist fight with you over her and you thought he was gonna tell you where his fucking nephew was, really dude", replied Kareem as he put his head down,

"You two niggas gone give me an aneurysm, fuck!"

Kareem got on his phone with Levi to get him up to date,

"Nigga, we got a problem."

Khori and Erica made their way to The Decatur Hotel, in New Orleans Downtown District, but Erica could see Khori was in a rush to get his bags up to the room.

"We in a rush to get somewhere?", asked Erica.

Khori slowed his pace as he turned to her,

"Nah, I just was trying to get our stuff upstairs and get comfortable."

Erica knew he was lying but she lead him on to believe she believed his story. Khori got all the bags in the room and headed to the balcony that looked over Downtown,

"I never took time to actually look at my city thru a visitor's eyes. It's really captivating how the Mississippi River truly makes the city what it is, with its curves and bends."

"I got your curves and bends over here", replied Erica as she walked up behind him,

"You act like you never seen the city before. I should be the one in awe, I only been here once and I was like 10 during Mardi Gras. You gone show me New Orleans or what?"

Khori walked back in the room,

"How about we rest today and Friday morning we head out and I can show you it all."

Erica had one question for Khori as she sat on the bed scrolling thru channels on the TV,

"So we gone just sit here and look at television all night?"

"I got a few ideas what we could do but I need to get in the shower first and clean up", replied Khori.

Erica laughed and started walking to the bathroom,

"You a lie, not before me but we could share the shower if you want to."

Erica went into the bathroom, leaving the door wide open and started the shower as Khori sat at the table. He could hear her in the shower and couldn't resist but to go see what that sexy body looks like unclothed. Khori walked into the steam filled bathroom and could see the sexy silhouette of Erica gracefully moving around in the shower. He started taking off his clothes to join her and the glass shower door opened with

Erica's hand out gesturing for him to come in. As Khori entered the shower her soft skin pressed against his,

"So you brought me over 300 miles from Houston to take a shower with me? We could have been did this a long time ago", smiled Erica.

Khori lifted her up with her legs wrapped around him, wedged her body between him and the shower wall,

"You was the one doing all the teasing not me."

Erica could feel his erect dick brushing against her parted pussy lips as the warm water ran down their bodies,

"So who teasing who, cause that shit poking my pussy right now."

Khori eased her down as he dropped down to his knees, put one of her legs on his shoulders and commenced to eating Erica's pussy better than she has ever had it done. His tongue rolled around her clit so good that Khori had her reaching for shit that wasn't there as if she was trying to brace herself. Erica's legs became weak as the subtle chills of her first orgasm creeped up her back and Khori could taste her delicious juices hit his tongue as she moaned out. He stood up and the two switched places as Erica pushed Khori against the shower wall, squatted down, grabbed hold of his harden man muscle and began to please him immensely with her mouth as the shower sprayed her back, the feeling was borderline magnificent. Khori had enough of her impressive oral pleasure and wanted to experience the rest of her luxurious body as he walked her out of the shower into the bedroom. They soaking wet bodies laid across the bed as Khori positioned himself between Erica's thick almond tone thighs. She could feel his stiffen manhood press against her moist lips and stopped him,

"Please tell me you have a condom. I so want this right now but…you know."

Khori got up, shuffled thru one of his duffle bags and satisfied her request with a three pack of condoms, as he smiled,

"We can start with this first and I'll go get some more later."

He put on one of the latex, got back in position and slowly entered Erica's warm moist waxed vagina. The two couldn't believe the amazing feelings they were encountering as the slow strokes increased into the hotel bed squeaking for help, sweat pouring from both of their bodies and moans of erotic pleasure filled the room, as the two climaxed simultaneously.

Jamal walked into his apartment to his daughter's laughter as she played with Garu in the living room. He seen his nephew and knew they needed a much deserve talk of the situation that occurred a few hours ago at his job. Jamal didn't want to believe his nephew had anything to do with the shooting he heard all over the news but he also knew Garu wasn't a "by the rules" kind of kid. Denise walked up to him,

"Baby you want me to fix you something to eat? I cooked some shrimp pasta."

"In a minute. Let me get outta these clothes right quick", replied Jamal as he stared down Garu sitting on the sofa.

Garu looked over his shoulder,

"Hey Unk, I didn't see you come in. This little girl is too active, for real."

As he looked in his uncle's eyes he knew something was wrong and instantly got up,

"You good?"

Jamal got close and whispered to Garu that they need to talk about Sunday at the fair. Garu had a feeling he knew what his uncle was about to say or ask him,

"Unk I left before any of that went down. I don't know who it was."

Jamal suddenly grabbed Garu by the sleeve of his shirt and pulled him into the back bedroom, the action caught Denise's attention because she never seen Jamal act that way toward his nephew.

"Nigga, Denise ex-husband came to my job asking about you! You wanna know why? Because the muthafucka has a witness or proof that you and your patnas shot his niece. What the fuck was you thinking? All the people in the city and you had to kill his niece", stated Jamal as he pushed Garu in the chest.

"Unk, it wasn't suppose to go down like that. I was going after Kush and the girl got in the way, I didn't even see her at first. That nigga been fucking my money up in Texas and I seen an opportunity to get rid of him and I took it", replied Garu.

Jamal stared at Garu with so much aggravation in his eyes,

"Yeah, you took it and now you got the damn Daniels looking for your ass. You stupid muthafucka! The more I teach you, the dumber I get."

Denise could hear the conversation from the room and couldn't believe what she was hearing. The young man that she so admired was responsible for the slaying of a very promising young lady she knew and loved, her heart was crushed. But what she heard next shook her to her core as Jamal started to tell Garu that he had to get out of the state for awhile until the whole situation blows over.

"Get whatever money you got saved up, I already booked you a bus ticket to Atlanta for tomorrow morning and you can stay with your uncle Raymond out there. I talked to him already so he knows you will be on your way there", stated Jamal.

Garu asked if he could stay at the apartment until he leaves in the morning but Jamal denied that invitation,

"Hell no! It's bad enough I'm doing what I'm doing but nigga you can't stay here. Go stay by your girl cause I know they probably watching ya mama house."

"Yeah, I can crash by Tiffany crib in The East tonight, you know 'Twin' and I'll head out in the morning to the station. Thanks Unk.", replied Garu as he walked out the bedroom and left the apartment.

Denise sat at the dining room table in total disbelief over what she just heard Jamal and Garu discuss. Jamal walked out the bedroom after he changed his clothes as if nothing happened,

"Where my plate at cause I'm hungry like a hostage baby."

Yolanda was in the kitchen cooking dinner when she heard Kareem walk in the house.

"Baby you cooked? I thought you wanted to go to the lil seafood spot today you was talking about", asked Kareem as he kissed his woman on the cheek.

Yolanda told him she wanted to stay in tonight, relax and chill while she dished up his plate. Kareem didn't mind staying home with her at all after his stressful day,

"To be honest that sound so much better cause after the day I had, I just wanna lay up under you."

Yolanda smiled as she brought him his plate,

"You just trying to get some of this here good good. You ain't slick."

Kareem shared an evil grin as he smacked Yolanda on her ass,

"Oh I'm a definitely get some of that good later tonight. Eat this food and then eat you for dessert."

The two sat down and were enjoying their dinner when Kareem phone started ringing but he was shocked when he looked to see who it was,

"Why Denise calling me? Hello. Yeah, I can talk. Stop playing."

Yolanda sat patiently at the table as she could only hear one side of the conversation but from Kareem's facial expression it was a serious discussion. She wondered what her sister had to talk to Kareem about because she knew it had to be something really important, they hadn't talked in years. Kareem thanked Denise, got off the phone and tried to eat his dinner,

"Shit! Let me text Levi real quick", stumbled from Kareem's lips.

Soon as Yolanda heard that name she knew that call wasn't a social one and her appetite disappeared as she got up from the table,

"Baby what's up with you and Levi? That dude ain't ever been on some legal shit and I don't need you getting caught up in his shit."

"Baby I just got him taking care of some stuff for me. Nothing to concern yourself about. I'm good, trust me", replied Kareem.

Yolanda got angered as she heard Kareem treat the incident so nonchalantly,

"I know you grew up with him but everybody that knows of him knows this dude is shady as shit and you got him coming out of your shop, texting him and now you having quiet conversations with somebody you haven't spoken to in years. What the hell is going on Reem and don't tell me nothing this time."

Kareem tried to just brush her off but Yolanda wasn't having it,

"Talk to me now or don't talk to me at all Reem. I'm not trying to get caught up in none of your shit."

"Can we just sit here and enjoy a good meal without you questioning me about dumb shit", responded Kareem.

Yolanda stormed out and went in the bedroom while Kareem sat at the table to try to finish his dinner but he couldn't. He got up from the table, walked in the room to see Yolanda sitting on the bed with tears in her eyes and he couldn't understand why she would be so upset,

"Baby what's wrong? It can't be all that just because you seen me talking to Levi. What's wrong?"

Yolanda started to tell Kareem about a past relationship she had with a guy she thought she would soon marry,

"It was way back when I was a teacher, I probably was like 22 or 23 years old, dumb and naïve and what I thought was in love. He was a gym teacher that was liked all over the school by students and other teachers but he was my boo. I knew he had his lil weed connect, shit what teacher didn't, but what I didn't know was that he was the plug for the whole school. Luckily we didn't stay together so when the police raided his apartment I wasn't there and they found 4 pounds of weed in his closet with a ledger of names. Needless to say beaucoup people got caught up in that shit. After that I promised myself I would never turn a blind eye to anything that don't seem right to me when it comes to someone I care about. Reem I love you dearly but I will walk away if you doing some illegal shit."

Kareem kneeled down in front of Yolanda ,

"Baby trust me it's nothing to worry about. Yes me and Levi use to run the streets hard when I was younger, shit we will always be connected. I did some shit back in the day that I am ashamed of and I probably sold your ex some weed cause that was many of my traits but I'm not in that life anymore baby. I've left all that shit behind me and I am definitely not going back to that. But if you must know, Levi found out who shot Ronnisha and I got him looking for the dude. Denise just called me cause she just found out who the guy is and told me where he might be. Now you know everything I know."

"Levi is gonna kill that guy if he finds him. Why didn't you just tell the police?", asked Yolanda.

Kareem looked her in the eyes,

"Really baby? They not looking for her killer. If anybody gonna find

Ronnisha's killer he will."

CHAPTER 8

Khori started getting dressed while Erica was what he thought was sound asleep but she set up to his surprise,

"Where you think you creeping off to dressed in all black? Most people with a black hoodie, black jogging pants and black kicks on at night don't wanna be seen. What, you think you a ninja or something?"

"Girl I just gotta meet up with my uncle real quick and I'm a be back", replied Khori as he kissed Erica on her soft lips.

He pulled the hood over his head, proceeded out the door, down the hallway and down the stairs to the courtyard. Khori knew Garu and his crew would be at a house in The East they call "the hangout" because it was tucked away from the main streets. He's been there a few times with friends and even on his own before all this animosity between him and Garu started. Khori knew the layout of the place, how the backyard was set up and even where they hide their stash. He just had to figure out a way to get in there without being seen. Khori drove down the Interstate without any type of plan but knew he had to get something done. He thought about shooting at the house but that would cause a near by neighbor to call the police. He thought about breaking the windshield of one of their cars but that would only bring out one maybe two guys when he needs all of them out of the house. Khori was stuck on a plan to get them out of the house but he kept driving. He finally made it to the hangout and to his surprise it was only two guys standing on the porch, no cars out front and no heavy traffic going in and out. Khori sat at the corner with his car off scoping out if anyone else would come out of the house but all he saw was those two guys. He figured Garu was inside hiding from him and the cops but Khori knew he had to get in that house. Then his chance came driving up the street, a big SUV pulled up and parked in the driveway of the hangout. The vehicle's doors opened up, five of Garu's guys got out with beers and what looked like grocery bags and they all went inside. He looked over the property and noticed two large garbage containers in front of the hangout, a distraction to get everyone out the house came to mind. Khori looked in his trunk, pulled out a half empty emergency gas can, some old rags and made his way up the street to the hangout. He quietly moved one of the garbage bins close by a window, opened it up, poured the gasoline in and lit the trash up. Khori rushed to the side of the house so that he wouldn't be seen and patiently waited while the blaze got bigger. A neighbor ran out his house from across the street and started frantically beating on the door of the hangout,

"Hey man! Y'all got a fire. Hey!"

All the guys came rushing out the front door and one guy yelled,

"Grab the hose pipe!"

When Khori looked he realized he was kneeling right next to the water hose, he quickly took off running and jumped the fence that led to the backyard, so he wouldn't get caught. He knew he had to move fast because he knew the fiery commotion up front wouldn't keep them all occupied for long, so he rushed in thru the back door with his gun drawn ready for anything. After Khori seen everyone was still outside dealing with the burning trash he searched around looking for a spot to execute his plan of attack. He thought about just waiting in the kitchen and having an all out gun fight with them but one 9mm against seven gunmen only works in the movies, he knew that would have a horrible ending. So he put on his latex gloves, pulled out the bag with the powdery ricin in it and looked for somewhere to put it so that everyone would be in contact with it somehow. Khori seen two large decorative hookahs sitting in the living room, removed the mouthpieces from the output hose and carefully poured the ricin in,

"Yeah, a nice inhale of this would do just fine. Yeah, get in there."

After returning the hose of the hookahs back in their original place, he sprinkled some dust on the food that was in the kitchen and immediately exited out the back door because he could hear the guys make their way back in the house. Khori stooped down in the shadows of the backyard as he listened to the crew laugh about the incident with the trash can,

"Man yo ass and them damn cigarettes gone be the death of us, ya heard me", stated one of the goons while he bit off of his poboy sitting in the kitchen.

"Say whoa, I didn't put my square out in the garbage", replied another.

Khori could see in the living room pass the kitchen and saw a guy stuffing weed in the hookah bowls as another started lighting them,

"You muthafuckas stop all that fussing like a couple of bitches and come hit this dro my nigga."

Khori seen his poisonous potion was being properly distributed as he planned and headed out the backyard to his car. He wanted to wait around to make sure everything works out as planned but he knew he had to get out of the neighborhood. He started up his car as he seen one of Garu's followers walk out on the front porch and sit down in a chair. He wanted to drive up and just shoot the guy because he recognized him from the fair on Sunday but he chose not to and trust in his venomous process. Khori drove off to head back to the hotel and Erica.

After his phone call with Kareem, Levi prowled the East of New Orleans in search of a girl named Tiffany, nicknamed "Twin". He never heard of her so he knew she wasn't in the game but if she's willing to hold Garu up for the night she's connected to some goons. Levi stopped at a well known strip club on Chef Menteur to see if he could grab some info on this mystery girl. He walked in the smokey club, found himself a seat and gestured for one of his regular girls to come over to him. The young half Black half Spanish dancer by the name of Cashmere smiled as she walked up to Levi,

"Hey Papi, I missed you" and sat on his lap all the while rubbing on his chest.

He enjoyed the attentiveness but Levi was there on business and got right to it as he slid a 50 in Cashmere's soft cleavage,

"That's cute and all babygirl but I need to find somebody. You know Garu right?"

The dancer nodded yes.

"Well I need to find a girl that's real cool with him. Her name is Tiffany but people may call her 'Twin', she stay out here in the East."

Cashmere thought a minute and remembered a girl she use to live next door to at The Frenchman Warf Apartments named Tiffany who was a twin. Levi listened as she told him all about Tiffany and her twin sister Brittany who use to live there with her but moved and also where the apartment was,

"You think she still lives there babygirl?"

"I just moved from there like a week ago, so she should still be there. Levi please tell me you not gone hurt her", replied Cashmere.

Levi looked at Cashmere with disappointment on his face,

"Have you ever heard of me hurting a female? C'mon now, that's not even my style. I'm just looking for somebody she knows."

"Well it looks like you working Papi so I'm a let you go", replied Cashmere as she leaned into kiss Levi on the cheek.

Levi got up and headed out to the apartments Cashmere told him about, he's been there before, so he knew the landscape and the hiding spots so that no one would see him waiting for his prey to appear because he was on the hunt. While he was sitting in the parking lot in front of Tiffany's apartment he texted Kareem to update him,

"Sitting out front waiting on this lil girl to show up."

Kareem just texted back with a "Thumbs up" emoji and Levi left the conversation at that. Levi knew Garu was leaving in the morning so he either had to get him tonight or in the morning when he leaves but the morning would be risky with people getting up to go to work, too many eyes. He waited for what felt like hours but it was only 20 minutes before he seen a glimpse of Garu standing on the balcony smoking a cigarette.

"There goes my bitch", Levi mumbled to himself.

He called a pizza delivery restaurant, told him he was a security guard at the apartment complex and ordered a large pepperoni while he put a plan together in his head. When the pizza delivery guy finally arrived, he walked up to him, paid for the pizza and politely sent him on his way. Levi walked up to Tiffany's apartment, with a large pizza in one hand and a .45 semi-auto in the other. He knocked on the door and he could hear rapid movement as he waited for a response. A young woman's voice came from the other side of the door,

"Who is it?"

"Pizza delivery", replied Levi.

The voice responded,

"Sorry, I didn't order a pizza. Wrong apartment."

Levi persisted,

"I'm sorry to bother you but the delivery is at this address. It's on the receipt."

The young woman again replied,

"I didn't order a pizza."

Levi tried one more time to get her to open the door,

"But ma'am your address is right…" and at that point the door swung open to Garu pointing a revolver right in Levi's face,

"Didn't she say she didn't order a fucking pizza bitch!"

Levi stared down the barrel of the firearm but wasn't phased one bit because Garu had done exactly what he wanted. All in one clean swoop, Levi dropped the pizza on the ground, grabbed the hammer and back end of the revolver, shoved his .45 right in Garu's mouth and walked him right back in the apartment. Tiffany screamed and started to run to the back bedroom of the apartment when Levi yelled for her,

"You need to stop right there, Tiffany!"

He then continued,

"Yes, your name is Tiffany and your twin is named Brittany. Now we can do this two ways. One, you run back there in the bedroom to do who knows what and I let the back of his head see the light of day all in your nicely decorated living room and then I shoot you in both of your kneecaps. Or two, you sit your ass down nice and quiet, I walk outta here with this dumbass and you never have to worry about me coming back to finish you off with this here cannon in my hand. So what's it gonna be babygirl?"

Tiffany sat down on the sofa next to her and didn't make a sound as she looked at the floor. The shock on Garu's face was evident with Levi's gun pressing on the back of his throat.

"Great job baby. Now me and Garu gone get up outta here because we got some things to talk about and you won't call not one person about this. If anybody ask you where he's at or where he went you just gone tell them he went to the bus station right? I don't want you to have to explain to Brittany why I'm in her house", politely articulated Levi as he turned Garu around and walked out of the front door.

The two guys walked to Levi's car as Garu silently looked around for any sign of anyone,

"I know you thinking of a way to get outta here, maybe you can run between the cars to get away from me, maybe you can take off running to the street but I want you to think about this first. I have a .45 semi-automatic with red tip hollow points in it, if you move in any direction I don't tell you to go in I'm a shoot you in the back, then I'm a drag you back to my car, put you in my trunk, shove this gun in your ear and pull the trigger til your head is no longer attached to your neck. Walk youngster."

Levi sat Garu in his backseat, duct taped his hands, feet and mouth and then covered him in a large comforter,

"Lay down and don't move."

Levi took Garu's phone out of his pocket along with his wallet and placed it in the front seat with him,

"Road trip time youngster."

CHAPTER 9

It's early Friday morning and Shalay woke up to hearing her twin's voice in the house talking to her kids. She pulled herself out of her bed to see what was going on,

"Why you making all this noise all early in the morning Lonna?"

Alonna looked over to her twin standing in the doorway,

"My bad sis, we taking the kids to the beach today to get out the house."

Lenelle ran up to her mother with the biggest smile,

"Mama, I'm going swimming, I'm a make a sandcastle, I'm a get on a surf board…"

Shalay started laughing at her little baby girl,

"Baby where you getting a surf board from?"

"We going to the beach. All beaches got surf boards", replied a giggling Alonna.

Cedric walked in with Sherell as he looked Lenelle in the eyes,

"Y'all ready? Cause I'm trying to go swim with the dolphins."

Lenelle's eyes got so big when she heard what her uncle just said and her little body bounced with excitement.

"Now see you gone have to deal with her looking for dolphins all day", replied Shalay.

Cedric just smiled,

"Me, Tre and Lenelle gone look for all the dolphins too."

Sherell shook her head as she laughed at Cedric's statement and went gave Shalay a hug,

"We taking the kids to Biloxi for awhile and you can have a nice quiet relaxing day."

Shalay welcomed the sudden adventure for her kids while she wrap her head around what's to come tomorrow. She didn't want to think about the upcoming funeral but it was literally the elephant in the room as she seen her family get together to head out. Cedric, Semaj and Lamaj loaded up the large van with coolers, towels and two beach umbrellas as Alonna, Steven and Sherell got all the little kids strapped in for the trip. Shalay watched as her family drove off and thought to herself that this is a perfect time to not be alone. So she texted Kevin,

"WYD, cause I'm in this house all by myself", as she started the shower in her bathroom.

Cedric was driving east to Mississippi when he told Lamaj he had something important to talk to him about,

"We gone talk later when we don't have so many people around us."

Lamaj just agreed and thought nothing of it because he had beach fun on his mind. The ride wasn't that long but long enough to have little Lenelle start to ask,

"Are we there yet? I don't see the beach. Where's the beach?"

Sherell tried to ease her little mind by telling her that they are getting really close to the beach but the little one's excitement wouldn't let her calm down. Right then Cedric caught sight of the beach,

"There it is!"

All the kids even the teenagers and adults got a little cheery when they seen the sand and the water. Cedric parked the van and everybody jumped out heading straight to the khaki colored sand that connected with the wavy waters of the Gulf.

"So nobody gone help me unload this stuff", asked Cedric.

Steven rushed over to give him a hand,

"Man them kids seen that water and forgot all about you and yo feelings."

They laughed as they carried all the items from the van to the spot the ladies picked out for everybody. Sherell was sitting on one of the large beach towels with Lenelle when she pointed over to Cedric,

"There goes Uncle Ced, go ask him baby."

Cedric looked a little confused because he didn't know what Sherell was talking about but he was about to find out because Lenelle was making her way to him. Lenelle's little 3 foot stature stood in front of Cedric with her hands on her hips,

"Uncle Ced, I don't see the dolphins. Where they go? You said the beach got dolphins."

"I'm sorry baby, the guy up front just told me the dolphins went to Florida this month and they won't be back until next month", replied Cedric as he looked over to Sherell weak laughing at his response.

Cedric and Steven ran out to the water with all the kids while Sherell and Alonna relaxed on the beach under the umbrellas. Tre and Lenelle were sitting right at the shoreline playing in the sand while letting the water hit their feet, Steven was throwing the football with Zachariah and Semaj,

Dashanae and Shantee were trying to see who could hold their breath the longest and Cedric took this time to be able to talk to Lamaj alone.

"Hey Manny, I needed to ask you something right quick", stated Cedric as he stood in the waist deep waters.

Lamaj was all ears,

"What's up?"

Cedric started telling Lamaj how he is proud of the young man he has become and how he really appreciates Lamaj letting him in his world. Lamaj thought it was a little corny that Cedric felt he had to tell him that but he let him continue to talk.

"Manny I'm saying all this to say, well ask you would it be ok to ask your mother to marry me today. I truly love her with all that I have but I really needed to get your approval first before I go any further", acknowledged Cedric as he looked a serious faced Lamaj in the eyes.

Lamaj's poker face instantly went away as he stated,

"Bout damn time! I'm tired of explaining to people, oh that's my mama's boyfriend and little brother. I would love to say, oh that's my step-dad over there."

The two gave each other a tight hug and joined the rest of the guys with the football in the water. Alonna was relaxing under the umbrella when she thought about her twin,

"Rell, I want to call Shay but I don't know what to say to her. I love my kids to death and I can't imagine what she's going thru right now."

"She knows we care and are there for her Lonna, we just need to give her some space and time right now cause tomorrow is gonna be rough for all of us", replied Sherell.

Alonna then told her that Delores still feels kind of responsible because if she didn't persist with them all being at the church that day that Ronnisha may still be alive. Sherell shook her head,

"That's nonsense. Mama needs to stop it. We all were enjoying ourselves and some ignorant fools came around destroying our happiness. She had no control over that, none of us did."

Alonna just laid there thinking of what ifs and maybes as she watched the kids play in the water with Cedric and Steven.

Everybody was sitting on the beach eating some cold-cut sandwiches Alonna made for the trip when Cedric gave Tre a small ring box and told him,

"Bring this to mommy. Go give it to mommy."

Tre walked over to Sherell and dropped the box in her lap as he walked off to finish eating his chips. She wondered where he found the black velvet covered box from but then seen Cedric kneeling in front of her. Cedric held onto her hand as he looked in her eyes,

"Baby I've been meaning to do this for a very long time. You are my world and I can't breathe without you. A day without you is an eternity without life itself. You've given me both of my sons and I can't thank you enough for that gift. We've taken it this far and all I see is infinite happiness if you do me the honor of being my wife."

The tears of joy flowed from Sherell's eyes as she listened to Cedric's proposal, delight filled her heart with promise of what she knew would be nothing short of greatness. Lamaj jumped up,

"Now that's how you fucking propose! Get it Pops!"

Everybody started laughing and Sherell looked over to her oldest son,

"Lamaj, watch yo mouth."

Alonna just hugged her sister-in-law so tight,

"I'm so happy for you baby. We getting married."

Sherell couldn't believe she was wearing an engagement ring from the love of her life and that Cedric acknowledge her oldest son as his own even though he's not biologically the father. Cedric looked over Alonna's shoulder and asked,

"So is that a yes or no?"

"I'm a have to think about this. I'm kinda cool with you just being my baby daddy, I don't know if you marriage material", responded Sherell as she let out the biggest smile.

   Khori was walking with Erica showing her the sights of the French Quarters and French Market. Erica was amazed at the old fashion architecture and how it stood the test of time,

"You telling me this cathedral been here since the late 1700's?"

Khori played the perfect tour guide for her as he showed her several old houses and pointed out how some of them still had the slave quarters under or behind the homes. He even brought her to historical cemeteries in the city,

"This the Voodoo Queen Marie Laveau's grave right here."

Erica looked at Khori with that "stop playing with me" look and backed away from the grave sight. Khori started laughing at her when his cell began to buzz but when he looked at the number he realized it was Detective Babineaux. His smile instantly disappeared and Erica sensed that the call was serious so she stepped back to give him space but Khori reached for her hand to be closer to him as he answered,

"Hello Detective."

Detective Babineaux wanted to find out if Khori was in town because he had some questions for him. Khori told him that he was close to Armstrong Park and he could meet him there, the two agreed as they ended the call. Erica was curious but she didn't want to pry into his conversation. Khori comforted all her curiosity by telling her that it was the detective in charge of his sister's murder and that he wanted to ask him some questions. The young couple sat on a bench at the front entrance of the park waiting on Detective Babineaux when Erica stated,

"After this you need to treat me to some dinner and I'm not talking about no burger and french fries either."

"Girl I know a place with the best burger and fries out here. But I guess I can splurge and get you a milk shake too", laughed Khori.

They started laughing as they debated on where to go and Detective Babineaux walked up to them,

"Hey Khori, how you doing today?"

Khori greeted him with a firm hand shake and the detective began to tell him why he needed to meet with him.

"I wanted to talk to you about something I encountered early this morning. I got called in to report to a house in The East about seven bodies found dead", acknowledged Detective Babineaux.

Khori had a good feeling he knew the exact house he was referring to but didn't give any clue he did,

"Ok, but why you telling me?"

The detective went on to tell him that a neighbor called 911 about a resident that was on the porch since late last night and hadn't move. When NOPD officers arrived they found an African-American male deceased in a chair on the porch but when they entered the home they found 6 other males all dead. After they searched the premises they found 2 pounds of marijuana, 5 handguns, 2 assault rifles and a shotgun. Detective Babineaux told Khori that three of the guns matched the caliber of gun casings found at his sister's murder and that they are being examined at the forensics' office now. But he also found out that two of the men that were in the home went to the exact same college as Khori but were not native to New Orleans.

"By any chance do you know a Michael Johnson or Patrick Boyd cause they both go to Texas A&M", asked Detective Babineaux.

Khori shook his head no but then Erica stepped in,

"Baby you do know them. That's 'J-Money' and 'Bird', they in our physics class."

"My bad, I really didn't know them by their real names", replied Khori.

Detective Babineaux then went on to tell them that they are still trying to figure out how the 7 men died but they are suspecting it was some kind of poisoning of some sort. Khori and Erica both had a confused look on their faces as Khori asked,

"Poisoning, like rat poison. Who kills people with poison? I thought that was just in the movies."

"You'll be surprised what people will do to commit the perfect crime", replied Babineaux.

The detective then asked Khori where he was last night,

"It's strictly preliminary that I ask you, especially because two of them go to your school."

"We checked in The Decatur Hotel like late afternoon and chilled the rest of the night", answered Khori.

But then Erica did something he wasn't ready for,

"Baby you remember we ordered room service too. It was my turn to pick and I had him looking at some girlie movies last night."

Babineaux took out his little notepad and wrote down what they both were saying,

"So y'all never left the room, cool. When forensics come back with the information on those three firearms, I'll be sure to tell you and your mother if any match from the scene."

Detective Babineaux thanked Khori for talking with him, went to his car and left. Khori looked at Erica with complete gratification in her actions and the only thing she did was expose them pretty dimples to him.

 Yolanda went to her sister's apartment to spend some quality time with her little niece Ashley but is still troubled over the Kareem and Levi situation. She just felt something was truly wrong with Kareem associating himself with a person like Levi and how he could lose everything if it goes wrong. Yolanda didn't want to go thru losing another lover to a criminal act that could be avoided. She walked up to the door and couldn't help but to smile as she could hear Ashley's joyous laugh from the other side,

"That lil girl is so loud."

When Yolanda rung the doorbell it swung open to Jamal standing there in his security uniform. Yolanda mauled over the notion that her sister Denise was only with Jamal because he was the father of her daughter and was always sarcastic to him when she sees him in his uniform,

"Good day Officer", as she saluted him like he was in the military.

Jamal ignored her actions as always,

"Baby I'm heading to work. I'll call you on my break" and walked out the door.

Yolanda laughed as she picked up her niece,

"He really don't like me, huh?"

"I wonder why? You always fucking with him", replied a giggling Denise.

The sisters sat down in the living room talking and playing with Ashley til she fell asleep when Yolanda had to ask her baby sister a serious question,

"Dee do you love Jamal? I mean like really love him, won't leave him, he's the one type shit."

Denise wondered why she asked her a question like that but if it's coming from her sister there's a deep reason why. Yolanda continued on,

"This shit with Reem getting close with Levi is really fucking with me. I know they been friends but they never been that close, well not since me and him been together. And you know Levi ain't nothing but trouble. If he getting involved in some dumb shit that's gone end him up in jail, I'm out for real."

Her little sister just sat there and listened to her vent but as soon as she heard Yolanda mention leaving Kareem she had to step in. Denise made sure Ashley was sound asleep first before she started talking,

"Girl Reem is not going to do anything that would endanger you, him or the family. That boy loves you something serious and he won't lose that. Now you asked me do I love Jamal. If you would have asked me that like two days ago I would have gave you a definite yes but now I'm trying to figure out a way to get me and my daughter away from this muthafucka . I know you know I called Reem the other day but do you really know why we had that talk?"

Yolanda was certain she knew all the details but when Denise told her who Ronnisha's killer was, where she knows him from and the actions Jamal took, the words floored her. Yolanda couldn't believe what Denise was saying,

"He wouldn't do that. He's an asshole but he can't be that cold-blooded can he."

"He knows I've watched that little girl grow up, he knew exactly who she was and that bastard sent that boy off to Atlanta to hide out from everybody. I hope Levi found Garu ass. Sat in my face like it was nothing. That boy and his uncle are fucking devils", replied Denise.

Yolanda started to reconsidered her thoughts after talking to her sister but still had doubts,

"I just don't want Reem implicated in none of that shit."

Denise then had a serious question for Yolanda,

"Sis, God forbid something like that happened to Ash. But if you knew who did it, you had someone that would take care of the problem for you and you knew where they were, you telling me you wouldn't try to do something about it? Reem love every last one of his nieces and nephews because he doesn't have any kids of his own, so he's gonna protect them at all cost."

Yolanda seen Denise's point and the thoughts of leaving left her but now she had thoughts of getting her baby sister out of the situation she's in.

CHAPTER 10

Garu woke up tied to a chair in a dark abandoned house, the only light coming from the sunlight peering through the old boards that partially covered the windows and Levi sitting at a table with an assortment of metal objects, cables, rope and a few other things he couldn't focus on. He attempted to scream for help but Levi shoved a wet towel into his mouth,

"Nah, I don't need you screaming, we didn't get started yet."

Levi went over to the table, picked up a heavy stainless steel chain, wrapped it around his right hand and ferociously punched the left side of Garu's face , breaking his jaw. Blood started to fill up in Garu's mouth as it slowly dripped out, at that very moment he knew he wasn't leaving the house alive. Levi dropped the chain on the floor and casually walked back to the table,

"You do know you killed the wrong person right? Now yes, I've done some diabolical shit in my day but I never involved anyone that's not part of the game. You young bucks truly said fuck the rules. Women, children, old folks and churches are off limits no matter what, no exceptions."

Garu tried to say something but the only thing Levi could hear was mumbles and groans,

"Yeah, I know. You sorry, you won't do it again, you didn't mean to. Yeah all that shit is fine and dandy but does it bring lil mama back, no."

Levi walked back to Garu in the chair with a hammer in his hand,

"But one thing you will do is apologize and I don't mean you saying you sorry cause you think you bout to die but because you really sorry."

Levi raised the hammer in the air with one hand as he raised up Garu's right pants leg revealing his shin and with a vicious swing struck Garu right below his knee. The sound of bone breaking sparked in the room and Garu's scream was muffled by the towel in his mouth.

"Did you know she was Shalay's second oldest? The cutest baby you'd ever see. That girl was a talented artist and had a promising future ahead of her. Did you know she was on the Honor Roll from Junior High all the way to Senior High? Smart as hell and gorgeous. But did you know, she was my daughter and only child?", asked Levi as he raised his shirt showing Garu a tattoo on his chest of baby footprints with Ronnisha under it.

Garu started crying cause he just realized he's locked in a house with the father of the daughter he was associated with killing. Levi looked him in the eyes and smiled,

"Aww, don't cry now. You too gangsta for that remember. See the thing is, everybody calls me Levi because that is my middle name. My first name is Ronald and I never really liked it so I had everybody call me by my middle name but Shalay loved my first name."

Levi sat back in a chair, lit a cigarette and began to tell Garu about how he use to date Shalay when he was younger. He told him that he was madly in love with Shalay and the love only grew stronger when his daughter was born but Shalay couldn't be around him because of his criminal background. The two went their separate ways but Levi tried to be present in Ronnisha's life, yearly birthday gifts, anonymous letters encouraging her to succeed at her talents, surprise gifts and money left in their mailbox on a regular basis. Levi always wanted to be more prevalent in everything Ronnisha was doing but he respected Shalay's wishes, she rather her daughter not know her father than know he was a criminal. While putting his cigarette out in Garu's hand, Levi even told him about Kareem,

"See I knew I had no chance in being close to my daughter but I needed my homie to have a relationship with his niece. That was the whole reason

I made him get out of the game and go his ass to school. Now look at Reem, big timer."

Garu started mumbling more and more to Levi as he told him about how he was trying to change his life around but the death of his daughter brought him right back to his dark side.

"You really trying to say something right now young buck", asked Levi as he slowly pulled the blood soaked towel out of his mouth.

"I'm sorry. I'm sorry", cried Garu as he looked in Levi's cold eyes.

"I know young buck. I know. I'm sorry too", replied Levi as he jammed a large carving knife in Garu's inner left thigh.

The pain was so intense that Garu didn't have a chance to scream before Levi shoved the towel back in his mouth.

"Yeah you bleeding heavy now, guess I hit that artery. We don't have much time left so I'm a make this quick before you bleed out", stated Levi as he grabbed a chrome .357 off the table.

He looked Garu in the face as he cocked the hammer back on the revolver and placed the muzzle of the gun under his left eye,

"You shot my baby girl in the face, my one and only child."

Levi closed his eyes thinking about the last time he seen Ronnisha's smiling face, inhaled deeply because he knew he would never see that smile again, the pain was unbearable as he slowly squeezed the trigger til the gun went off with a loud bang. The job was done and the only sound that could be heard in the house was blood dripping on the floor as Garu's head emptied out.

Khori and Erica was waiting on the valet from the restaurant to show up with his car when he got a text from Devin,

"WYA cuz? I need to talk to you."

Khori tried to ignore the message but he knew if he didn't answer him soon he was going to get a call. Khori replied,

"Chilling with Erica right now. What's good?"

Khori was getting in his car when Devin called him,

"What up cuz?"

"Did you hear about J-Money and Bird?", replied Devin.

Khori didn't really want to talk about what he heard about the incident,

"Yeah, I heard about it."

Devin was surprised how uncaring Khori was on the phone,

"Nigga, you know J and Bird are always with Garu but they didn't mention him. Where the fuck is he?"

"I don't wanna talk about this shit over the phone, damn! Meet me later at the hotel. I'm a call you when I'm there", replied Khori as he hung up the phone.

He was visually agitated after he got off the phone with his cousin,

"Fuck!"

Erica had to get a better insight on the situation as she made herself an accomplice when she lied to the detective,

"I know you got a lot on your mind but what the hell is going on? You and me both know J-Money and Bird are part of Garu's crew and that the rest of those guys in that house probably part of his clique too. Kush, what the hell did you do last night?"

Khori looked at Erica as they sat at a red light,

"You don't wanna know. But they deserved whatever they got."

Khori started driving around the city looking around Garu's old stomping grounds in search of maybe a glimpse of his rival or someone that knows him. He wanted to drive back around to the hangout but he knew it would look real suspicious if he drove through that neighborhood after talking to

Detective Babineaux. They were driving through Lake Pontchartrain area when Erica couldn't take the silence anymore,

"Bring me back to the hotel, please", stated an upset Erica.

Khori looked over to her,

"What's wrong with you?"

"You got me all the way fucked up. I'm in this car, you ain't say one word to me but 'you don't wanna know' since we got in and you been driving around the city for the past 30 minutes. I done put my ass on the line, lying to the cops for you and you acting like I'm not even here in the car. So do us both a favor and bring me back to the hotel", replied Erica.

Khori knew he had messed up with her as he pulled over to park and tried to make up for his actions,

"Look, I know I put you in a fucked up situation and I can't say thank you enough for covering for me with that detective but I don't want to get you any more involved than you already are."

Erica responded with extreme conviction,

"Boy, I can't be anymore involved than when I became your co-conspirator by telling that man you was with me all night. Now like I said before, I know it has to be some bullshit with Garu because he didn't go anywhere without J-Money or Bird and for them two to be dead it's some serious shit."

After listening to Erica make her point, Khori finally opened up to her and told her everything starting with that horrible day his sister was murdered. He told her it was all his fault that she was killed,

"If I didn't show up that weekend Nisha would still be here."

Erica tried to assure him it definitely wasn't his doing but the actions of Garu but it couldn't change the pain he was feeling. Khori got out of the car to walk to the edge of the lake and sat at a bench. Erica made her way to him when he stated,

"Ronnisha painted a picture of the lake back when she was like 12. My mama was so amazed by it that she showed it to everybody that would look, then a guy seen it that lived in Atlanta and bought it. We found out later that the portrait was featured in The Atlanta Press, people all over the South wanted this little 12 year old originals. Nisha was even featured in The Times-Picayune for Upcoming Young talent of New Orleans. My lil sister was so gifted and they took that from us."

Erica sat there trying to console Khori the best she could but she never experienced the feelings he was going through but one thing she did know, he wanted Garu dead for what he did.

"I gotta come clean and tell my mama. She's gonna hate me for being responsible for her daughter's death but I gotta tell her the truth, this shit is eating me up", explained Khori as he got up from the bench,

"But if I can't see my sister's smile anymore, that bitch Garu gotta cease to exist."

"I got ya back 100% cause if somebody killed my little sister I would want to do the same as you. But you gotta be on the up and up with me dude. We been knowing each other since freshmen year, shit you know my background better than some of my female friends", replied Erica.

Khori knew she was telling the truth, Erica was the first person on campus he met besides his counselor and the two immediately connected, with classes together, school games and several parties. But the bond grew stronger when the two were at a frat party, where Erica had entirely too much to drink, passed out in a lawn chair in the backyard and Khori caught a guy trying to take her clothes off while his buddy watched. Khori beat both of the guys with a tennis racket and took Erica back to his dorm where she woke the next morning completely dressed with Khori asleep on the floor. At that moment she knew she could trust him no matter what and now she needed him to know he can trust her just as much.

Kareem was sitting in his living room looking at cartoons with Ashley while Yolanda and Denise were chatting it up in the kitchen.

"Y'all just gone leave me in here looking at these puppets?", asked Kareem.

Denise walked in laughing at the sight of Kareem planted on his leather sofa with Ashley firmly seated on his lap,

"I'm sorry Reem. Let me get her."

"Leave my baby alone, she chillin'. But you two not gone leave me in here to watch this by myself", replied Kareem.

Denise sat down next to him and laid her head on his shoulder as she watched how good Kareem was with her daughter,

"Reem, you really need one of your own."

Kareem chuckled as he pointed at the TV,

"What? A puppet? I don't know how to talk without moving my lips tho."

He always thought about having a child but he and Yolanda were still fresh in their relationship, having a baby was never a conversation they brought up.

"C'mon, think about it. You could have a little Reem Jr running around here or Karen if it's a girl", smiled Denise.

Kareem looked at Denise with the most disinterested look,

"Girl you still talking. What we need to be talking about is why this show got this girl in a trance, she ain't move."

Denise just smiled with the sweetest reply,

"Cause she been sleep since I walked in here. She is so comfortable with you, Reem."

He couldn't believe he's been sitting watching a children's show all that time,

"You gotta be kidding me. She lucky she cute or I'd wake her up."

Yolanda walked in from the kitchen,

"Gimme my baby. I'm a go lay her down in y'all room."

As Yolanda picked Ashley up and carried her off to the guest bedroom, Denise had a chance to seriously talk to Kareem. She looked down at the abstract patterned area rug that was under the wooden coffee table in front of them,

"Reem, I know this shit is really awkward for you and I really appreciate you letting us stay here awhile. I promise we won't be here long. I know you're gonna say don't worry about it and take your time but I need to get me and my daughter our own place. But I just wanted to say thank you."

"Girl if you don't stop that mushy shit. You and Ced not together but that don't mean you not family. Now shut up, cause I think this puppet trying to build a rocket ship", replied Kareem.

"You really still looking at this, really Reem", asked a laughing Denise as she realized that was just his way of saying "everything's ok", a strong caring trait from the Daniel's family, something she truly missed.

Yolanda walked in and sat next to Denise,

"You do know you can change the channel now? She not in here."

Kareem and Denise looked at each other and burst out laughing.

CHAPTER 11

It's early Saturday morning and the day couldn't be anymore

gloomy for the whole Daniels' family than it is today. The sun seemed to

refuse to show as an array of different shades of gray nimbostratus clouds

covered the sky. Delores was gathering her things together as she got

ready to leave for her granddaughter's funeral, a day she never thought she

would have to experience. Cedric was helping Lamaj with his tie while

Sherell was putting Tre's shoes on, the house was morbidly quiet. Kareem

and Yolanda were already at the church with Denise and Ashley because

Kareem wanted to make sure that Mr. Bordelon took care of everything

his mother wanted, the funeral director happily went over every detail with

Kareem. Alonna knew where she needed to be, right next to her sister and

Shalay welcomed the company. The twins sat in her room as Shalay

attempted to get dressed but the sorrow of today brought on so many

emotions that weakened her to the point where Alonna had to help her

sister button her blouse. Steven and Kevin were in the den with the kids

while Khori, Devin and Erica waited outside. Khori tried his best to stay

strong, refusing to show the slightest bit of sorrow but the thought of

what's to come battered him to no extent. Kareem sat in the second row of pews, eyes fixed on the Mother of Pearl colored closed coffin, completely motionless and oblivious to everything around him when Cedric sat next to him. The brothers had no words for one another, their eyes spoke for them with nothing but pain, sorrow, hurt and anguish as Cedric just sat next to his little brother. Cedric looked over to Yolanda sitting with Denise and Ashley, it shocked him to see Denise there but pleased him all the same.

"She's staying with us for now because she doesn't feel safe or comfortable staying with Jamal", stated Kareem.

"Yolanda is family and any of her family is family too", replied Cedric.

The church's double doors opened to Delores walking in, the Daniels' monarch seemed to float across the hardwood flooring of the temple and was met at the end of the row of pews by her sons. She embraced them both with a hug and kiss on the cheek as she looked at the coffin that held her precious grandchild.

"Where's Yolanda?", asked Delores.

Kareem pointed over to her as he told Delores that Yolanda wanted to sit out of the way of the family and allow them all to get their proper seating. Delores turned and gestured for both of the women to come sit with her,

"Those girls are family too. Hey, one of them still holds our name and maybe later the other one will too", as she turned and looked at Kareem with a smile.

That smile from their mother simply alleviated a lot of what was going on, like a soothing ointment would an open wound, it was still there but now it's a little more bearable.

Sherell walked in with her boys to seeing Denise sitting next to Yolanda with Delores and her sons. She was actually satisfied that Cedric and Denise put their differences aside for a greater good at being there for the family as she and Lamaj sat next to Cedric. Tre made it his purpose to sit close to his grandmother because she always have sweet peppermint candies in her purse for him when they're in church. The hall started to fill up with its congregation but Khori still hadn't made it inside yet. He watched as his mother and siblings went in but fear froze him to the sidewalk. The sound of the choir singing started to bellow out to the street, gospel vocals echoed out of the double doors, when Levi walked up to Khori,

"Why you not inside, lil homie?"

Khori ignored Levi's question and started walking away from him because he never seen Levi before, besides Khori wasn't in the mood to talk to a stranger.

"Damn, it's like that Khori? You gone just walk off on me", asked Levi.

Khori was caught off guard when the stranger knew his name,

"Say man, who is you?"

Levi laughed at how Khori looked at him,

"Calm down, it's all good. Damn, you got bark like a pit."

Levi started to tell Khori how he been knowing him since he was a baby. Khori's attitude started to ease as he found out this stranger knows his whole family and even grew up with his uncles.

"Say man, you asking me why I'm not inside. Why you not", asked Khori.

"It's complicated but I do need you to do something for me. Give this flower to ya mama and tell her Ronald said he's very sorry", replied Levi as he handed Khori a White Tiger Lily.

Levi knew it was Shalay's favorite flower and when they were dating he would always bring her a dozen, especially if she was upset or mad. Before Levi walked off he gave Khori some advice,

"Go in there, say goodbye to your sister and pay your respects. She deserves so much more lil homie."

Khori knew the stranger was telling him the truth but his feet felt like they were full of concrete when he attempted to cross the street. He was halted by a horse drawn glass hearse carriage that pulled up in front of the church. The carriage was trimmed out in pink roses and ivy vines, followed by a brass band and accompanied with 6 motorcycle units from the Sheriff's department. The church began to empty out as people started to fill the sidewalk and street, Khori had missed his sister's entire funeral service. He pushed through the crowd at the door of the temple, making his way to his family that was all gathered in front of Ronnisha's casket with Pastor Jenkins. Khori stood next to his mother, handed her the White Lily Levi gave him and told her what Levi had said. Shalay turned around looking to see if Levi was in the church,

"Where did you see Ronald?"

"He was outside, mama I gotta talk to you about something", replied Khori.

Shalay could see the pain in Khori's eyes and she could feel that it was something really important to him. Khori, Devin, Semaj, Cedric, Kareem and Lamaj all stood on the sides of the coffin with their white gloves on to carry Ronnisha outside. Shalay didn't know what Delores had put together because she wouldn't tell her but when the doors to the church opened wide and the Daniels' men carried the casket out, you could hear the low sounds of horns blowing. The brass band were playing on the side of the glass hearse and when the door of the hearse opened, 16 white doves came flying out. It was like the Heaven spoke because as the doves flew up in the air, the gray gloominess clouds seem to part and the sun shined through. The Daniels family slowly loaded the coffin into the hearse as onlookers cried for the family's loss. The hearse began its slow journey down the street with the family, band and followers close behind as the motorcycles blocked off crossing streets. Shalay seen her oldest son was truly bothered,

"Baby what is it that you wanted to talk to me about?"

Khori heart sunk into his chest with fear but he needed to get his problems off his spirit. He began to tell his mother how Ronnisha's demise was his fault and the person who was responsible for the shooting. Khori even told Shalay how he went looking for revenge on anyone that was involved with killing his sister. The whole time Khori was talking, Shalay was hoping the whole ordeal was a dream and that she wasn't listening to what she had just heard. The fact that her son had brought danger to her family and as a result her oldest daughter paid with her life stunned Shalay to her core. She didn't know how to handle the situation, she didn't know if she should be disappointed in her son, mad at the ones who killed her daughter or happy that her son was honest with her. Shalay had to evaluate it all on her own but she didn't realize she had distanced herself from her own child by stepping away from him in the crowd and walking directly next to the hearse with one hand holding onto it. Khori simply let his mother walk away because he knew in his heart she was completely upset with him, for what he did and he didn't blame her because he was upset with himself.

Kareem and Cedric were walking on the side of Delores, who was seated in a golf cart, following the procession when Kareem seen two smaller groups joining the crowd. He could see big signs that had pictures of Ronnisha on them followed by Mardi Gras Indians in full gear. It was a sea of rainbow colored feathers and beaded costumes walking along side of the glass hearse carriage.

"They told me they were gonna make it and they did", announced Delores as she smiled at the sight, "My baby loved seeing The Indians."

The arrangement Delores put together with Mr. Bordelon all came to fruition as they came to a stop at the grave site. Ronnisha's coffin was lowered into the ground as Shalay silently watched trying to hold herself together, she walked to the edge and dropped the White Tiger Lily on top of the casket. Khori tried to hold his mother's hand but she slowly pulled away from him not even looking him in the face. That simple action tore Khori soul apart, to him his own mother wanted nothing to do with him. Khori quietly walked away from the burial, off on his own, heartbroken. Erica seen him and immediately followed suit,

"Khori wait."

Khori stood in front of a large mausoleum that was dated in 1911,

"I wonder if their family didn't want them around. I wonder if they did something to disappoint them. My mama can't stand me right now."

"You told her? Trust me, she still loves you baby. She's just hurting right now", replied Erica.

She could see Khori was broken and she tried her best to help him through this rough time. Khori looked across the mass resting place of several people and focused in on a male image standing in the distance, it was the stranger from earlier,

"That's that dude again. Who the hell is he?"

Khori walked up to Levi this time but was met with stern advice,

"You in the wrong place youngin'. You suppose to be over there with ya mama, she needs you right now."

"Dude, you don't understand. She don't want nothing to do with me", replied a tearful Khori as he asked, "Again why aren't you over there but I have to be."

"Like I told you before, it's complicated. Your family has a bond like no other, through faults, mistakes or bad decisions they will always come back together. But know this, I'm not part of your family but your enemies are my enemies and it has been taken care of. Get over there to them Khori", replied Levi as he turned and walked away through the graveyard.

Khori made it back to the burial site right when Pastor Jenkins was finishing his sermon, he could see his whole family standing across from him and right at that moment felt he could never be a part of that union. Khori felt it was all his fault they were all in agony and his best option was to separate himself from them all. He removed the white gloves he used to carry his sister's casket, dropped them in the grave with a pink rose and walked off telling Erica,

"I'll be at the hotel. Call me when you're ready for me to come get you. I can't be here."

Devin watched his cousin walk away but knew he couldn't go after him and he gestured to Erica to go with him. Khori walked back to where his car was, head down and devastated at what was going on in his life.

In New Orleans a funeral has two parts, the first part is the time for mourning that the person has passed, sometimes with a band playing low solemn music but the second part is the time to celebrate their life with the band playing loud celebratory songs of happiness and this one was no different. The brass band that followed the march to the burial site with the family, lead the march back to the church horns blaring loud tunes of joy as people danced in the street celebrating Ronnisha's life. Shalay was saddened but at the same time overjoyed that so many people came to support her and her family. Kareem and Yolanda "second line" down the street with family and friends as Alonna and Steven danced with the Indians. The twins' children joined in the celebration while Tre sat on his grandmother's lap in the golf cart. Cedric and Sherell danced along with everyone else back to the church but were stopped by Denise who congratulated them on their engagement. Denise then did something neither of them expected,

"Ced I just want to apologize for how I been acting, I was a total bitch at times and it was all my fault. Sherell, you got you a good one. He's

stubborn as shit but he has a heart of gold and all he wants is your love.
I'm really happy for y'all."

While everyone was celebrating, Lamaj went back to say his own personal
goodbye to Ronnisha but stopped because he seen this man kneeling in
front of her grave. The sounds of the band echoed down the street but
Lamaj could hear the man talking,

"We never got chance to connect but I truly wish you knew I was always
there for you. I love you babygirl, daddy loves you."

Levi stood up, wiped the tears from his eyes and walked pass Lamaj to his
car.

"You're her daddy?", asked Lamaj.

Levi turned around as Lamaj continued,

"She always talked about you to me. She knew her mama didn't want her
to meet you for some reason but she couldn't wait til she turned 18. She
looked forward to letters and gifts from you. Man she really loved you,
she really did."

The words coming out of Lamaj's mouth healed Levi's pain like a
soothing warm blanket. Levi never expected the words from a teenage boy

would be the words he needed to hear. He got in his car but before closing his door he thanked Lamaj for what he told him,

"I heard great things about you lil man. I'm looking forward to seeing you and your cousin Devin on the football field."

"Thank you sir", replied Lamaj.

After watching Levi drive off, Lamaj turned to talk to Ronnisha,

"I met your dad. He seems to be a cool guy. It hasn't been a week and I miss you so much. I'm standing here and I really don't know what to say. Nisha, I love you and I miss you, this shit hurts so much. You not my blood but that don't mean we wasn't family. Love you Nisha."

Lamaj walked off and headed back to the church.

Kevin was walking Shalay to her car after the crowds started to clear,

"I'm a head home, ok. So you and the fam can have y'all time together."

"Kev, I need you there. Please come over", replied Shalay.

Kevin happily agreed, caressed Shalay's cheek and gave her a kiss as he closed the car door,

"Everybody meeting at mama Dee house right? I'm a be there baby."

Kevin was walking back to his car when he seen Cedric and Sherell standing next to their car, waiting for Lamaj to get back, with two of the biggest smiles he ever seen from them. Kevin figured they just seen what happened,

"What? Why y'all standing there looking like matching goof balls?"

"What's good brother-in-law", laughed Cedric.

" I knew it. I knew it", shouted Sherell all the while pointing at Kevin like a court prosecutor.

Kevin was getting in his car when Lamaj was walking up,

"Say, Kev when you gone let me drive that monster? I'm getting my license this year."

"You gotta say Uncle Kev and he might take you on a ride", replied Cedric.

Lamaj had a puzzled look on his face but before he could get out a question, Kevin loudly replied,

"Can we please go now. Y'all play to much."

CHAPTER 12

Khori was sitting at the hotel's bar with Erica drowning his sorrows in a bottle of Cognac. Erica didn't want him to take the route he was taking to get over his situation but she understood he was hurting and he simply was trying to numb the pain. Khori appreciated that she was there with him and felt it was no better time for them to really get to know one another than the present.

"Ok, I know college Erica. I wanna know the real Erica. What was your childhood like", asked Khori.

"Where do I start? I grew up in Southwest Houston with my little brother and little sister. My mom was a prostitute and my dad was her pimp. They got arrested on a human trafficking sting and I moved in with my grandmother on the Northside where I got into several fights with girls and gangs. Ended up in juvie for 9 months and then that's when I realized I didn't want to be like my parents. So I straightened up, focused on school and got myself a scholarship", replied Erica.

Khori looked at her with disbelief,

"Girl stop playing, you serious?"

Erica giggled as she took a sip from Khori's glass,

"You can't make this shit up. I'm not saying I had it super hard but it wasn't easy. Shit, I almost followed in my parents' footsteps when I got busted but the judge showed me some mercy and just sentenced me to 6 months in a private placement. Trust me the carefree Erica you know has some skeletons that I refuse to allow to come out."

They sat there talking about their childhood and Khori even told her how he got involved in selling marijuana. How he and Garu were real cool with each other in the beginning and that when he first created Hulk 2.0 he went to Garu first. Garu turned him down, saying it won't sell because it looks comical, so Khori created Kush and the product blew up on campus.

"After school I really wanted to get with a dispensary somewhere and start my own company, maybe have my own growing fields", stated Khori.

Erica agreed with him,

"That would really work for you Khori, you're really good at what you do. People flock to you for your stuff. So that's what we doing after graduation?"

"We? When did this become we?", asked Khori.

Erica leaned in and whispered in Khori's ear,

"It became we when you put my legs on your shoulders and put my pussy in yo mouth."

Khori did something he hadn't done in days and that was burst out laughing.

"Why don't we head upstairs and see if you can find something to put in my mouth", replied Khori.

Erica got up from her chair,

"Oh, I got a lot you can use that mouth on but I gotta take a shower first."

Khori looked her in the eyes,

"Girl I am your washcloth."

"You so damn nasty", laughed Erica as they headed to the elevators.

Kareem was sitting on his mother's porch while everybody was inside when he received a text from Levi,

"I dropped our friend off at the Atchafalaya River, looks like he's gonna stay there. See y'all in a few weeks."

He thought that text would make him feel better but the fact that he was sitting at his niece's repass was still a dagger in his heart. Cedric walked outside by Kareem,

"You got that text from Levi? This shit still don't feel good bro."

Kareem took Cedric's phone from him and stomped on it,

"Tomorrow morning, report your phone lost. Say you lost it at the funeral, something, we don't need anything coming back to us."

Cedric agreed,

"I love you lil bro. C'mon, lets go inside."

Delores was so busy making sure everyone had everything they needed that it just dawned on her that Khori wasn't there. She went to Shalay,

"Baby, where's Khori? I seen him at the funeral but that was it."

"Mama I don't know where he is and I don't care. I can't deal with Khori right now", replied Shalay.

Delores looked at Shalay with utter concern,

"I don't know what he did or said and I don't care but you just buried one of your children, don't lose two in one day. Shalay you have done plenty of things that disappointed me to my soul but I stood by you no matter what."

Shalay just shook her head,

"Mama you don't understand. I appreciate your concern but I don't know if I can forgive this. Now don't get me wrong, I love my son but I need time."

"Don't let that time be decided at a gravestone. It's too late to resolve a problem when one of the people can't respond back. Give me my flowers while I'm still alive, is all I'm saying", replied Delores as she walked off to tend to her grandkids all huddled around her cakes on the kitchen counter.

Sherell, Yolanda and Denise were all sitting in the backyard sipping on some wine when Yolanda laughed,

"It is crazy how tragedy will always bring black folks together. I'm not trying to bring up no bull but I would have never thought I would see this day."

Denise rolled her eyes at Yolanda,

"Girl you play too much, shut up. Me and Sherell pass that."

Sherell laughed as she thought to herself,

"I been pass it. You was the one still holding on to bullshit."

Alonna walked in the backyard where the ladies were,

"What you heffas doing back here? Y'all got me stuck inside with the dudes and all them kids. Denise, Ashley is so freaking cute. I just wanna get all the sugar from her."

"You can have her, she bad", replied Denise.

Yolanda quickly responded,

"My baby is not bad. She's just behaviorally challenged some times."

The ladies all laughed at Yolanda's comment when Sherell pointed out what she saw earlier today,

"So nobody seen Kev and Shay kiss earlier today?"

Everybody stopped laughing and were fully attentive to what Sherell was saying. She then told them how her and Cedric were waiting for Lamaj when they seen Kevin walking Shalay to her car.

"He opened her door and when she sat down they started lip locking and I ain't talking bout a peck on the lips either", stated Sherell.

Alonna was a little shocked but thrilled for her sister,

"That heffa ain't tell me nothing about them. I'm not gone say nothing right now."

"Y'all know Shalay been crushing on Kev. Shid, I'm surprise it took this long", replied Denise.

The ladies laughed and gossiped about the issue but got silent quickly when Delores came outside to check on them,

"You girls doing ok out here? Y'all need anything?"

"We good mama, go sit down and relax", replied Alonna.

Delores' next statement stunned everyone outside,

"I think Shalay and Kevin doing it, for real."

Everybody exploded in laughter at the elderly woman noticing with her own eyes what they had been gossiping about out back.

"Mama!", shouted Alonna.

Delores gave her an angelic face,

"What? I'm just saying, they real buddy buddy. More than usual. Just how Yolanda and Reem was before they let everybody know."

Yolanda`s face blushed red in embarrassment,

"Mama Dee, stop it."

Delores accomplished her task in cheering everybody up like she always does and walked off back in the kitchen,

"Semaj! Get out that pot with yo fingers!"

Sherell just giggled,

"That lady there is something else."

"A total character, I tell ya", replied Denise,

"But you gotta love her."

  Shalay was sitting on the sofa being consoled by Kevin when little Lenelle walked up to them,

"Mommy why you laying on him like that and why he holding your hand?"

"Little girl mind yo business", smiled Shalay.

Kevin picked Lenelle up and sat her on his lap,

"I was just holding mommy's hand to help her feel better baby."

Lenelle leaned back and rested her little head on Kevin's chest,

"Mommy, you feel better?"

Shalay interlocked her fingers with Kevin's and rested her head on his shoulder,

"I do now baby."

Cedric viewed the sight and was completely pleased to see his sister smile again after a truly trying time. He looked at Kevin and gave him a defining nod of approval but as his best friend Cedric had to mess with him,

"Brother-in-law, you good over there? You straight?"

Kevin started laughing but countered Cedric's comment by kissing Shalay,

"I'm all good bro, all good."

Dashanae walked up to Alonna who was still sitting outside,

"Mama, grandma got like beaucoup balloons in her room."

Alonna looked puzzled at her daughter's statement as she got up to see what Dashanae was talking about,

"Mama, what's the balloons for in your room?"

"What balloons?", replied Delores.

Dashanae took Delores' hand and walked her to her bedroom,

"These balloons grandma. Mama talking bout these balloons."

"Oh Lord, I forgot all about them. We was suppose to release them in the air", responded Delores.

She had Steven get everybody to go outside in the backyard as Cedric and Alonna brought the balloons outside. Everyone was handed a balloon and Delores started in prayer,

"Almighty, we come to You as Your humble servants. Our precious child is resting in Your loving arms, safe from harm and no pain but we miss her so. Lord, we send these balloons up to Ronnisha as a gift to her spirit to let her know she will always be in our hearts and minds. Lord, watch over her mother at this time and heal her heart. Lord, watch over this entire family and protect them. In Jesus mighty name we pray. Amen."

Everybody released their balloon and they all floated away in the breeze like a pink cloud.

After watching the balloons disappear into the sky, Shalay seemed to distance herself from the crowd by walking back inside and heading out the front door. She just wanted to have some alone time to think about all that she found out today, she wanted justice for her daughter but she didn't want to have her son put away. Shalay felt if she didn't call the police with this information it would be like disrespecting Ronnisha. Shalay was definitely stuck between a rock and a hard place when Alonna came outside to check on her twin,

"You okay sis? I seen you walking back and forward on the porch."

Alonna could see her sister was bothered but it wasn't a look of sadness this time like earlier today. Shalay sat down on the steps of her mother's porch,

"I found out why Nisha was shot and who did it but if I tell the police I'm a lose somebody close to me."

"Is saving somebody ass more important than getting justice for your daughter", asked Alonna as she sat next to her sister,

"They wasn't thinking about you when two of your children were being shot at. Fuck them, call the police. If you can't, tell me who they are and I'll call the police."

Shalay thought about how it would all affect her family but she wanted justice for her daughter. After a deep breath, Shalay then went on and told Alonna what Khori told her, Alonna was floored. She couldn't believe what her sister was saying and that her nephew hid this from everybody. Alonna got up and went inside looking for Devin because she knew he had to know something. She found Devin sitting with Kareem and Cedric at the kitchen table,

"Devin come here."

Devin knew just from his mother's tone it wasn't anything good and jokingly replied,

"Mama, I ain't do it."

Alonna stood over Devin,

"Where is Khori? I know you know. And why didn't you tell me?"

Devin looked confused at her questions,

"Tell you what? Last I seen Khori was when he left the funeral."

Alonna tried not to get loud because she didn't want to alarm everyone in the house.

"Khori told his mama about Garu and what happened at the church that Sunday", stated Alonna.

Cedric overheard Alonna mention Garu's name and he knew he needed to gain control of the situation before it gets out of hand. Cedric whispered in Alonna's ear,

"Come with me outside. We need to talk."

As they both headed for the front door, Cedric called for Kareem to come with them. When they got outside Shalay was still sitting on the steps but she was talking on the phone at the time. Cedric and Kareem waited until she got off the phone because they wanted both of their sisters to hear what they had to say. Alonna was impatient as she paced the porch,

"Cedric what do you need to talk to me about?"

Her comment caught Shalay's attention as she put her phone down and asked,

"What's wrong?"

Cedric sat down as he gathered the strength to speak,

"I want y'all to know first off, we didn't try or want to hide this from you but we knew y'all wouldn't agree with our solution. We found out from a friend what happened Sunday and who was responsible, we had it taken care of because we didn't want Khori arrested."

"What the hell you mean taken care of", asked Alonna.

Kareem just looked at his sister with the most serious stare,

"Lonna what do you think? That motherfucker killed my niece and if it wasn't for Denise's help, he would have gotten away with it. So yes, it was TAKEN care of."

Shalay couldn't believe what her brothers were saying but what was really bothering her was what she had to tell them.

"The thing is, I just left a message for Detective Babineaux to call me cause I have information about my daughter's case", stated Shalay.

Cedric's body seemed to just drop in his chair after hearing what his sister said.

"Why Shay", asked Kareem. Cedric mind rambled as he thought about what was going on with the case and remembered about the two guys that the detective called Shalay about,

"Didn't Babineaux tell you that those dudes he found went to school with Khori and Devin? Well when he calls you back, tell him that your nephew told you they use to always hang with this drug dealer named Garu and that's the info you had for him."

Shalay and Alonna reluctantly agreed to their brother's request but also knew it was the only thing to do. Cedric and Kareem went back inside to talk to Devin and prepare him for a possible phone call from the detective.

CHAPTER 13

Khori woke up to Erica cuddled up next to him in the bed, it felt amazing having her there but it was checkout time and they had to head back to Texas. He started rubbing her arm,

"Time to get up sleepy head, we gotta go."

Just the sound of Khori's voice made her smile as Erica stretched herself, getting up from under the covers. The two began packing their luggage when Erica's phone started ringing but when she looked at the screen she didn't recognize the number, so she did like most people and ignored it. Khori grabbed everything as they went to the elevator, the cute couple just embracing this new relationship feeling as she leaned into him and Erica's phone started ringing again.

"Who is this 504 that keeps calling me", asked Erica as she showed Khori the number on her phone.

He recognized it was Devin calling and answered,

"What's up Dev?"

Devin replied agitated,

"Dawg, I been trying to reach you all morning. Ya phone keeps going straight to voicemail."

"I turned it off cause I didn't feel like being bother at the time. What's good, wha cha need", replied Khori.

Devin let his cousin know that he was just checking on him because he hadn't heard from him since the funeral and was just a little worried about him. Khori appreciated the call but was kind of distant,

"I'm good cuz. I just gotta get my head straight, take some time away, ya heard me and see what I'm a do with myself. I'm a keep in touch with cha soon. Love ya Dev."

Devin ended the call but was a little bothered with how his cousin sounded, Erica noticed the cold tone also but waited until they were in the car before she said anything. She sat there and finally asked,

"Baby, you ok? I know the shit with you and your mother is messing with you but you sound like you literally cut all ties with that phone call."

Khori's eyes were fixed on the road as he replied,

"I just gotta focus on my shit, get all my stuff in line. Just like you said, I'm good at what I do and that's exactly what I'm a do."

"Khori, I understand that but don't cut your family off in the process. Your family is what makes you, you", replied Erica as she held onto his hand.

He was listening to what she was saying but Khori was headstrong like his mother and once his mind was set, it was no stopping him. Erica had two options, let him go or come along for the ride either way he was moving forward and leaving his past behind him for now. It was going to be a hard adjustment but Khori felt it was the best option for him and his family.

Devin was getting his things together before his trip back to school when Dashanae walked in, sad face and all.

"What's wrong with you", asked Devin as he stuffed clothes in his suitcase.

"I hate it when you leave", replied Dashanae while sitting on Devin's bed.

"I'm a be back in a month and for Thanksgiving and Christmas. I promise I will call or text you everyday", replied Devin.

He went to his car with his luggage in hand after kissing his mother and hugging his siblings goodbye. Devin was sitting in his car getting ready to pull off when Steven walked up to his window,

"You be safe on that road, ok. I'm a see you later boy."

Devin let out a slight grin when he replied,

"Thanks pop, talk to you soon."

Devin never called Steven that before and that statement touched him more than Devin could ever imagine. Steven smiled and reminded Devin,

"You my best man next month, we gotta do it big. You got my back?"

"Always pop, always", replied Devin as he drove off.

Yolanda and Denise were sitting in the backyard watching Kareem chase Ashley around when Denise stated,

"He is so good with her. Do you know that girl wakes up looking for Reem in the morning?"

Yolanda just sat back looking at how attentive Kareem was with little Ashley and Denise could see her sister was mentally somewhere else.

"Londa, what you thinking about like that", asked Denise.

"Oh nothing, just looking at how he is with her and thinking how great a father he would be to this one", replied Yolanda as she rubbed her stomach.

Denise nodded her head yes at the statement but then realized what her sister had just said to her. She jumped out of her seat,

"Stop playing! I know you lying! For real?"

Yolanda just laughed at how excited Denise was for her,

"Yes, I'm for real."

The joyous display caught Kareem's attention,

"What's wrong with you, saw a lizard or something?"

Denise was bubbling with excitement when she replied,

"Nope not a lizard."

Her giggles and smiles made Kareem laugh aloud at her actions but he still didn't know what had Denise so happy, so he asked Yolanda,

"What is wrong with yo sister? She on that shit?"

"No silly, she just happy cause I made her into an auntie for the first time", replied Yolanda.

Kareem looked at her in total shock,

"Baby, you serious? We pregnant?"

Denise shouted,

"YES!"

Yolanda replied to Kareem,

"I don't know about if we pregnant but I do know I'm 10 weeks right now."

Kareem was at a lost for words as he stared into his woman's smiling eyes.

Shalay was coming back from a hike thru the walking trails at City Park, to get her mind right, when she was heading back to her car to a surprise. She seen Kevin and her kids waiting for her,

"What are y'all doing here?", asked Shalay.

Kevin told her that he and the kids wanted to have a picnic with her at the park. Shalay welcomed the gesture with a gracious smile as she gave Kevin a kiss.

"Lenelle and Shantee seem to like me but I don't think Zach cares for me always being around", stated Kevin while he was getting a cooler from the trunk of his car.

"He has always been protective over me", replied Shalay,

"That's my little man."

They were relaxing close to a bayou where the kids found some ducks to feed bread crumbs to as Kevin and Shalay watched. Kevin was telling Shalay how good the maid service, they operate together, was going since she's been absent when she had to stop him. Shalay didn't want to spoil the pleasant outing but she had to ask,

"Kev, what are we doing? Where is this going? Cause I don't really know. I mean, I really appreciate you being there for me when I needed you but what are we really doing?"

"Well it looks like we enjoying a nice picnic with the kids, that's what I thought we were doing", replied Kevin.

Shalay looked at him,

"Kevin Talport, you know what I mean."

"Dang, you gotta call out my government name. Well to answer all of your questions, my parents wanted to have dinner with us tomorrow night cause my mother wanted to meet this Shalay I talk about so much, if that's alright with you. Plus, I have someone very special to me that I want you to meet. I told you the first time we kissed that I want to be your everything, that I want to just be part of you and I meant every word of it. Baby, I'm not going nowhere as long as you and the kids would have me", replied Kevin.

Delores' neighbor Mrs. Evans called Cedric, concerned about her aging neighbor,

"Hey Cedric baby, I'm just calling you cause I think you need to check on your mother."

Cedric couldn't imagine anything was wrong with his mother, being that he was just there last night.

"What's wrong Mrs. Evans?", asked Cedric.

"I heard her arguing in the backyard but when I looked over the fence to check on her, it was just her back there. I asked her if she was alright and she said she was fine but she called me Katherine", replied Mrs. Evans.

Cedric knew Mrs. Evans' first name was Barbara and that his grandmother's name was Katherine. The statement caught him off guard but he knew it probably was just a simple mistake and assured Mrs. Evans he will call his mother real soon. After Cedric got off the phone with Mrs. Evans he immediately called his mother,

"Hey mama, you ok? I was just checking in on you."

"Oh baby, I'm doing just fine. Just sitting here looking at my stories", replied Delores.

Cedric was kind of relieved that his mother sound normal over the phone as they held a pretty decent conversation about the kids, her garden and even Mrs. Evans' little dog using her flowerbed as a bathroom. He was getting off the phone with her when he stated,

"Ok mama, I'll talk to you later. Love you."

"Love you to Reem, tell Ced to call his mother sometimes", replied Delores.

Before Cedric could respond she hung up her phone and he figured it was just another simple mistake that she called out the wrong name, but was it...

OUTRO

It has been almost two years since Ronnisha's funeral and Khori pushed himself harder and harder everyday. He graduated from Texas A&M with Honors in Botany and didn't even attend his own graduation. He mailed his cap and gown to his mother, weeks before, with a copy of his diploma in a frame with no return address on it. The family tried everything to get in touch with him but he kept his distance. It seemed as if he just vanished but Khori moved to Colorado with Erica right at his side, keeping him grounded, where he did what he always talked about doing and that's join a marijuana dispensary. But Khori's products got so mainstream and popular that he had to start his own dispensary to keep up with the demand in multiple states. Business was booming, he was doing what he loved and he had someone there to share the entire experience with but Khori was still unhappy. He knew he could have all the riches in the world but nothing could fill the void of that family love he so desired.